SOME LOSE
THEIR WAY

SOME LOSE
THEIR WAY

Frederick J. Lipp 7033

A MARGARET K. MCELDERRY BOOK

Atheneum 1980 *New York*

Library of Congress Cataloging in Publication Data

Lipp, Frederick J
Some lose their way.

"A Margaret K. McElderry book."
SUMMARY: Newly friends, following a long period
of enmity, Vanessa and David, both outsiders,
study bird life in The Bottoms and the effect in-
dustrial pollution has on the birds.
[1. Friendship—Fiction. 2. Birds—Fiction.
3. Pollution—Fiction] I. Title.
PZ7.L6646So [Fic] 80-13510
ISBN 0-689-50178-1

Published simultaneously in Canada by McClelland & Stewart, Ltd.
Manufactured by R. R. Donnelley & Sons, Inc.
Crawfordsville, Indiana
Designed by Maria Epes
First Edition

For Marian

Here a star, and there a star,
Some lose their way!
Here a mist, and there a mist,
Afterward—Day!

—EMILY DICKINSON

SOME LOSE
THEIR WAY

Prologue

DAVID said, "I've got something for you, Vanessa."

Nick and Eddie were standing on either side of Vanessa so that she could not get away. The grins on their faces were about ready to explode. There was no expression on Vanessa's face. Vanessa never showed anything.

And that, for David, was the idea of the game: to get through to Vanessa, to — just once — make her pale, frozen face show something. It was a challenging game because he had not yet won at it; it was becoming a serious game because he did not like losing.

"Hold out your hand," he said.

"No," she said in a little voice.

"It won't hurt you. I promise."

"No."

"Okay." He sighed. He glanced at Nick and Eddie. They grabbed her arms. Nick bent her left arm behind her; Eddie forced her right arm out, palm upward.

David laid the fat dead mouse in her palm.

Vanessa began to scream.

"Score one for our side," David said, smiling faintly. Eddie was breaking up.

"I told you she hated mice," Nick gasped. Vanessa was still screaming.

David took the mouse from her hand and tossed it over

3

the playground fence. "Let's go," he said. "Here comes old lady Maxwell."

"What's the matter with Vanessa?" Miss Maxwell demanded.

"I don't know," David said. "All of a sudden she started screaming!"

The screaming went on even after they took her into the school. She quieted, though, after the nurse gave her a pill. The rest of that day, however, David heard the screaming go on in his mind. It filled him with shame. The next day he almost went up to her and said I'm sorry. He would have done so had it not been for the way she looked at him. The look deepened his shame; it made him feel as so many things did so often — thoroughly sick of himself.

As the days passed, and the look did not leave her eyes, he grew angry with his feelings. He began resenting the look. He started teasing her again, thinking up ways to make her life miserable.

He could not understand why it seemed to make his own life that way too.

Chapter 1

VANESSA saw him waiting for her near the end of the alley. Where it was too far for her to run back, and where there was no way out except past him.

She knew then exactly what would happen and how it would end. She had walked down alleys like this in the other places where she had lived. Not always alleys, of course. Sometimes they were streets; once it had been a long, narrow passageway between two stores. But in the end it seemed always like one big alley that never changed.

Always at the end someone was waiting.

This time it was David, and there wasn't much she could do about it anymore. She was afraid of him, he knew she was afraid, and she had grown weary of living through day after day in this kind of afraidness. This time she would keep on walking, let it happen once and for all, and get it over with.

For it had to happen.

One afternoon several weeks ago — it was after she had begun staying after school to help clean blackboards and sometimes help grade papers — Miss Maxwell had come into the room and looked at her thoughtfully for a few moments.

"It's four-thirty, Vanessa," she finally said. "Shouldn't you have gone home long ago?"

"I won't be much longer, Miss Maxwell."

"What I mean is — you're a wonderful help to me, and I do appreciate it. But shouldn't you be out playing with the other children?"

"I like doing this. It's fun. Besides, I don't have to be home right after school."

"Is that the real reason?"

Vanessa put on her cool, casual face. "What else?" she said.

Miss Maxwell frowned. She went to the window and looked out. "I think you'd better tell me about it," she said.

"About what?"

"Whatever the trouble is."

"There isn't any trouble, Miss Maxwell."

Miss Maxwell turned from the window. "Vanessa. I've been a teacher for nearly twenty years. That means lots of schools, lots of classes, it means hundreds upon hundreds of students. It also means that I have a sixth sense for trouble, the kind of trouble children your age find themselves in. And my sixth sense tells me that you're having trouble."

Vanessa shook her head.

"I don't know what it is, of course. But I have the feeling it has something to do with the fact that you're younger than the rest of the class, and physically smaller, and because of this you're picked on quite a bit. I have the feeling that lately it's been getting to you."

"No, Miss Maxwell. Honestly . . ."

"You know this. I know it. Now what I think we ought to do is bring it out in the open and talk about it."

"But there's nothing to talk about."

But there was. And Miss Maxwell had finally gotten it

out of her. And the next morning, David had been called out of class to the Principal's office. And that afternoon Vanessa had seen him again, white-faced and wretched, accompanied by a large angry man who must have been his father, both of them waiting outside the principal's office. After that, David had not come near her until now.

Now . . .

The alley stretched ahead of her. It was May, and the sun was bright. The alley was filled with sunlight and shadows, and robins were calling up and down its length. It was hard to believe that anything was about to happen to her.

Then it was not hard.

She watched him walk slowly toward her. She hugged her books tightly. They were strong and solid, and she felt herself very breakable. Perhaps by holding fast to the books she would not be broken.

He stopped in front of her.

"You can relax," he said in a very quiet voice. "I'm not going to touch you. I'm not going to do a thing to you. Not now. Not while school's on. But I want you to know something. You got me in big trouble. At school and with my father. And when school is out I'm going to get you. I know where you live, and I'm going to be laying for you. You might think you're going to get away with this, but you're not. Sooner or later I'm going to get you. And when I do, you're going to wish you'd never been born. Got it?"

He walked away.

Vanessa waited a few moments until she had stopped shaking, then went on. At the end of the alley she turned into the long main street, which seemed to run on forever above the river.

It was called Front Street and along its one side were

old-fashioned store fronts with little old-fashioned houses and duplexes in between. You could tell by the store fronts what kind of neighborhood it was. That is, there was one small grocery store and one small drug store. And nine taverns. There was also a store-front church, a bowling alley and two pool rooms; finally there were pizza and hamburger and taco-eating places with names like Dominick's and Burger Boy and La Hacienda. All these were on the right-hand side of the street.

On the left-hand side were the plants. First, the shipyards. Then the crushed-stone plant. Then the blast furnaces and the steel mill and the storage yards piled with mountains of rusting scrap. And where these ended, the refineries began: the squat, massive storage tanks, the mysterious skyscrapers of pipes and tubing, the towers with jets of burning gas that licked the night like torches. The plants and refineries ran along a high ridge above the river.

Below the ridge, stretching out to the river's edge, lay The Bottoms, an overgrown jungle of woods and thickets. In a clearing of this jungle was an immense pit, larger than a city block and deep as a quarry, which was diked all around with high earthen walls. Like The Bottoms, the pit was a waste place, a fill basin for the muck pumped into it by dredges deepening the river channel. Accidents had happened there. Worse things than accidents. Never, Vanessa had been cautioned, go down into The Bottoms. Never even go near there. Not that she needed such warnings. A combination of fear and good sense kept her away.

Altogether, The Bottoms, the refineries and blast furnaces, and the mixed black and white neighborhood around Front Street amounted to a kind of world. It was not much of a world, but if it was what you had, you got along in it.

Although there were times, Vanessa thought, when it didn't seem worth making the effort. Times like now.

She watched the girl walking slowly toward her in the window of Kovach's drug store. All at once she decided to pretend it was not her own reflection in the window but that of someone else. She closed her eyes, erasing everything. I am a stranger, she said to herself. I am walking down the street. Now I am going to see "Me" for the first time. She opened her eyes and looked into Kovach's window.

The stranger was small and very thin. She had a blonde pony tail and was hugging her books desperately, as though she thought they might save her from something. She was funny-looking too: her dress too long, her cardigan too large, her arms and legs poking out like skinny branches. She had a little clown face, a little stub nose spattered with freckles, and a pale little fringe of bangs almost resting on her eyebrows. The only large thing about the girl was her eyes: they filled most of her face like eyes painted on an Easter egg. That was what the face of the girl in the window was like — an egg face or a clown face. It would probably never be anything else, so there was no use even pretending about it. She walked on past the window, ignoring the girl.

But it wasn't just the face, she thought. Or being little and on the funny-looking side. That was only part of the trouble. The real reason was that she didn't fit anywhere. There was no place she really belonged. That was the trouble with skipping grades, her grandmother said. It moved you ahead too fast, before you were ready for it. Gram hadn't wanted her to be skipped, but the principals in the schools had insisted. "She should be with her own mental age group," they said. So they had moved her ahead. And because they had, she had always been younger and smaller than everyone else in each new grade. And what this did was, it made you a kind of freak — too young for the kids in your grade, and too old for the kids your own age.

In the end, like now, you wound up in the eighth grade only because you had eighth grade brains. The rest of you was somewhere behind. "Brains are no good, Vanessa," Gram would sometimes say. "Not for a girl anyway. All they do with a girl is make her different and lonely."

Which was true, the lonely part anyway. But not altogether true. Because there was Gram.

And no matter how far outside things she might be in school, there was always an *inside* to come home to, a place where she belonged. And every inside, in all the towns they had ever lived, had always been filled with Gram. And love. So there was Gram. And now there was also Charlotte — who wasn't so much a neighbor as she was family.

Her black family, as Vanessa liked to think to herself.

Char lived next door in their double-sided house. In a way, it was like one of those crazy weather boxes you sometimes saw, where a little old lady came out of one door when it was going to be sunny, and a little old man came out of another door when it was going to storm. Only in the weather box of Gram and Char and herself, it didn't matter who was in or out because it was sun all the time. So — to be really honest about it — she couldn't say she was lonely at all.

School? Forget school; that was tomorrow, a long way off. Between now and then . . .

She ran the rest of the way home, up the porch steps, two at a time, and swept open the door. "Gram, I'm home!"

She was about to call out, "You know what happened to me today?"

But didn't.

Because Gram came slowly toward her from the kitchen. Not smiling. Not saying a word. Only looking at her.

Chapter 2

$\mathcal{A}LL$ at once the room seemed very still. And darker than it should be.

Gram took her face gently between her hands and tilted it up. She kissed her on the forehead. "Vannie," she said. Vanessa waited for her to say what was wrong, but she didn't. She merely drew her fingertip down the bridge of Vanessa's nose. "Fifty-eight and three-quarters freckles," she said.

"Sixty," Vanessa replied. It was a game they played between them. It meant nothing but love.

Vanessa gathered her courage. "Is something wrong, Gram?"

"No."

"Something's the matter. I know."

Gram turned suddenly and marched into the bedroom. She closed the door, but not soon enough. On the bed Vanessa saw the overnight case and garment bag, and the small, neatly stacked pile of clothing. She caught her breath.

Time seemed to stop.

Only her heart went on beating.

She scarcely ate any supper that night. Sometime later she heard her name called and went into the parlor. Gram was sitting in the large wing-back chair. "Come sit with me, darling," she said. "There are some things we have to talk about." Vanessa scrunched into the chair. She took her grandmother's hand between hers and held tightly.

"Uncle Mart called this afternoon . . ."

Vanessa nodded. Uncle Mart had married Aunt Rachel, Gram's other daughter. Uncle Mart and Aunt Rachel lived in West Virginia, had six children, and weren't supposed to have any more because Aunt Rachel was sickly. But they were having another. Vanessa knew the rest.

". . . and you know how they're fixed, Vannie. Uncle Mart's never had what you could call regular work, so they can't afford help. And there's only so much you can expect friends and neighbors to do. So I've got to go. There just isn't anyone else and your Aunt Rachel needs me."

Vanessa did not look at her grandmother. "I need you too."

"I know that, Vannie."

"Aunt Rachel has Uncle Mart and the kids. I don't have anybody but you."

"I know that too. That's why this whole thing is so —" Gram stopped as though she couldn't find the words. She shook her head helplessly. "I don't want to leave you. It's the last thing I want. I've been trying all day to think of some other way to work this out. But there isn't any way. You know how small their house is. There isn't room for me, let alone both of us. And with Aunt Rachel sick, and all the confusion — No, there's no other way, Vanessa. I don't want to leave you here, but I can't take you either. Not at first, anyway. If it looks as though it's going to be long, then I'll send for you. We'll have to find some way. But for now — until I get there and see how things are — I'm going to have to leave you here."

"Alone?"

"No, you're going to stay with Charlotte."

13

"I'll be alone, though. Char works during the day —"

"But you're at school."

"— and she goes out lots at night."

"You'll read and watch television like you always do."

"I'll be alone." It seemed to Vanessa that she could not quite grasp the fact.

"You won't have to worry about money. I've arranged with Mr. Schilling at the bank to cash both the pension and social security checks. And Charlotte knows how to handle everything."

"I'll be alone."

Gram drew her close. "Vannie, Vannie, what am I going to do?" Her voice rose, broke.

Vanessa felt her grandmother's body tighten like some powerful spring; she could feel the spring growing tighter and tighter. And all at once she thought: *If I were going away and leaving Gram, I would feel the way she does. And if she were acting like me, she would only be making things worse.* The thought came. And went.

But changed everything.

It seemed to her, suddenly, that she was the stronger of the two, and that in some way it was Gram who was the child and needed to be comforted. And to do this, Vanessa knew she had to grow up quickly. "I know, Gram," she said. "You can't help it." She even managed to smile and actually say, "I'll be all right. Don't worry." And because her grandmother remained like an anxious child, refusing to be comforted, she went on saying it in different ways until she almost came to believe it herself. I *will* make out, she thought. Somehow.

Later, after she had washed and shaken out her pony tail and said her prayers and curled herself at last under the covers, Vanessa thought about it.

Being brave — it was supposed to be a good thing. But it

14

didn't stop things from happening to you. It didn't stop you from being an outsider, or being left alone when your grandmother went away. It didn't stop people like David from doing what they wanted to you. It didn't stop anything.

All it did was add an extra weight on you that, no matter how much you wanted to, couldn't be put down.

Charlotte padded across the floor in her bare feet, wearing a housecoat with a pattern of furious purple and red flowers crushed over it. With the housecoat, and her rich mahogany skin, and her pink hair curlers sticking up like electric light plugs all over her head, she looked like Topsy grown up. Her grin was a big Topsy grin.

"You know anybody around here named" — she glanced at the envelope in her hand — "Miss Vanessa Elizabeth Dunlin?"

Vanessa went along with it. "Never heard of her."

"Neither did the mailman." She handed Vanessa the envelope. "Only name mailman knows you by is Vannie, so I took it for you. Looks like it's from Gram."

"Thanks, Char." She opened it quickly and scanned it. What she wanted the letter to say was, "I'm coming home." Or, "I'm sending for you." Or at least, "We'll be together soon." But all it said was that Gram had arrived after a long and tiresome bus ride. And that it was good she had, because Aunt Rachel's house was a mess and the kids were running wild and Uncle Mart didn't know how to cope with anything. The letter ended "Love" and "I miss you," both of them underlined three times. But that was all. The only good thing about the letter was the name on the envelope. It looked interesting, written out in full like that. It looked important.

Miss Vanessa Elizabeth Dunlin.

Charlotte was taking the curlers out of her hair. "What does she say?"

Vanessa shook her head. "She's not coming. And she's not sending for me."

"She will, Vannie. Don't worry 'bout it."

"I'm not worried. It's just that . . ." She shrugged. There were no words for the emptiness the letter had brought.

"I know. You miss Gram. You was hoping."

"Well . . ."

"— and even though we're friends, it ain't the same." With the curlers out of her hair, Charlotte wasn't Topsy anymore, she was herself. She was real.

"We're not friends, Char; we're more like family. You could be like my big sister or something."

"Or something is right." Charlotte laughed suddenly, a surprisingly giggly sound. "We're like an ice cream cone, Baby: chocolate and vanilla."

"Double dip."

"That's us." Charlotte glanced in the mirror and picked up her hair brush.

". . . Char?"

"Mmm?"

"Was Susie, was your little girl like me?"

"Crazier."

"Little?"

"Littler."

"Did she ever grow up — I mean get taller?"

"She's tall as me now. Almost."

"Where is she now?"

"Chicago." Charlotte stopped brushing. "Susie teaches school in Chicago. Josh is in the army. Rose is still down in Memphis — she got married last year."

"You must have got married awful young, Char."

"Too young, Baby. I wouldn't do it again. No." She began brushing again, long strokes that crackled. "Don't you do it either. You wait till the right time."

"When is the right time?"

"You'll know."

"Is it the right time for you now?"

"What does that mean?"

"I mean — you know — like you go out a lot. Your gentleman friends, Gram says."

"That's a nice way to put it." She laughed delightedly. "Yeah, it's a good time for me. Fact is, that's the big trouble with me, Vannie. Seems always to be a good time."

She went on brushing her hair. It grew longer. It was like watching someone painting a picture, Vanessa thought. The hair growing longer, the face softer and higher, everything changing moment by moment. Only Charlotte was doing it all with a hair brush.

Vanessa said solemnly, "You know something, Char?"

"What?"

"Like they say — black is beautiful. It really is." She touched the blue-black hair; it wasn't stiff, the way it looked sometimes, like black steel wool. It was soft as her own. "You are anyway."

Then suddenly it was June, and the last day of school.

David approached her as she was clearing out her desk. He looked down at her and smiled. "I'll see you one of these days, Vanessa," he said. She did not understand the smile. "Incidentally," he added, "the mouse won't be dead the next time. And it won't be just a mouse."

From then on she began hiding.

It was not that she hid in the house or in any particular

17

place. It was only that something inside her became very careful and watched where she went. Something inside her became as wary as though she actually hid.

And in hiding, there was nothing to think about except the piece of fear in her mind named David.

It was a funny kind of fear in a way, something she could almost see and feel. It was hard and black like a piece of coal. It didn't do anything; it just lay there. The only way to stop thinking about it, she knew, was to keep busy.

But there was nothing to do. That was the problem.

Each morning when she awakened, she made the bed and hung up her clothes — which took care of her own bedroom. Then she made up Charlotte's room. After breakfast, she washed the few dishes, straightened the sink and carried out the trash — which took care of the kitchen. Nothing was ever messed up too much in the other rooms, but even so, she made a point of dusting them.

But none of these things took long to do, and afterward there was only the long day stretching ahead.

She was afraid to go to the playground or the park because of David. But even if there had been no David and nothing to be afraid of, it wouldn't have been much use. The kids there were all those who played and hung around together in school. All those who had somebody else. And as for the television — after a few days of it, all the daytime serials began sounding the same, and the same guests seemed to be making the rounds of all the talk shows. Television was part of all the nothing.

And so she read.

She would have read anyway, even if Gram had been there. But not so much, maybe, or so long. Or with such concentration. The library was nearby too, and there were

18

certain backyards and alleys she could cut through to it without having to worry too much about David. When the library opened each morning she was there. When it closed she carried an armful of books home and read through the evenings when Charlotte was gone.

She read swiftly, hungrily. Good books, bad books; dull books and stupid books. She read anything and almost everything. In a way, there was no sense to her reading.

"This one," Charlotte said, picking up *David Copperfield*. "I didn't read this till I was in high school. And you're reading it now." She shook her head, the pink curlers swaying. "You're too smart for your own good, Vannie."

"No I'm not. I just like to read, that's all."

"You don't do anything *but* read."

"What's to do, Char?"

"Play. Horse around. Get out in the sun and get dirty. But then that ain't your thing, is it, Baby?

Vanessa shook her head. "I'm some kind of nut, I guess."

She went on reading — except, of course, when Charlotte was at home. Those nights they would watch television together, and pop corn. And talk.

"Too many women around you," Charlotte would say sometimes. "That's your trouble."

"Just you and Gram. That's not too many."

"I mean like a father, or brothers. You should know how to mix it with menfolk."

But that was silly. A father? Brothers? She couldn't even imagine what it would be like. Her father had run off before she was born; her mother had died when she was three. Whatever need she might have had for either had been filled by Gram. Even now, she thought, with nothing but books and Charlotte, she was making out all right on her own.

19

One day Miss Matasek, the librarian, came to her table with a book. "I suppose you know all about Camelot, Vanessa?"

Vanessa looked at her, puzzled.

". . . Arthur, Lancelot, Guinevere, the Round Table —?"

"No, Miss Matasek."

"Then it's about time you do, and I don't know any better way to begin than this." She put the book down. It was a thick book, the kind Vanessa liked because thick books were like worlds you could enter and live in for a while. The book was called *The Once and Future King*.

She entered into its world.

Six hundred and thirty-nine pages later, when she closed the book, it was as though she had closed the door on some real and beloved kingdom and on people who had become as living — and dear to her — as Gram and Charlotte. She could not bear leaving them. Like that day, walking home from the bus station and knowing Gram would not be there. It was like that with the people in the book.

There had to be a way back to them. It couldn't end just like this.

She took the book back to the library.

Miss Matasek smiled at her. "How did you like it, Vanessa?"

"It was wonderful." She sighed. "I've never read anything like it."

"I'm so glad."

"Miss Matasek —?"

"Yes, dear?"

"Is there anything — I mean are there any other books about, like King Arthur and Camelot and — you know . . .?"

"Oh my yes. All kinds of books. Have you read . . .? No, of course you haven't. I think now, though, perhaps —

if you're really that interested — you might try Malory. He's the one who wrote the original story. Yes, I think you're ready now for Malory."

And so there was Thomas Malory and the *Morte d'Arthur*. And then there were other books. Books after books about knights, about kingdoms, about whole worlds of lovely enchantments. Reading was sometimes like a long happy dreaming from which she would waken from time to time, and then return to dream on.

"Tune out, turn off — that's what you're doing, Baby," Charlotte complained.

"No I'm not, I'm just reading."

"But you're missing so much out of life. It just breaks my heart."

"I'm not missing anything, Char. This is what I like doing."

"But all the time? Honey, whenever I see you — whenever — it's with your nose in a book. You're never with the other kids. All you're with is books."

"That's okay with me."

"It's all on account of this kid, David, ain't it?"

"No."

"Don't give me that. I know about these things. You're scared of him and that's why you're laying 'round the house all the time reading."

"I'd be reading anyway, Charlotte."

Charlotte sighed. "It's too bad you ain't black, honey, or you ain't got a little black in you. 'Cause if you was black, even though you was a girl, you'd stand up to this kid and punch him up a little and get the whole thing over with."

"No I wouldn't."

"You poor baby, you."

"Don't say that. I'm not a poor baby."

"You just don't know how poor, that's all."

"It makes me feel awful when you say that."

"All right, I won't say it anymore." She lit a cigarette. "It's like I say, Vannie, over and over — and it ain't your fault. You got no mother, no father. You just got Gram. And I love her, you know that. But Gram's too old to be raising up a girl your age, growing up like." She blew two thin jets of smoke through her nostrils. "Maybe you're looking for something in them books you read. The people you don't have. Who knows? I don't. You don't either, most likely. All I do know, Vannie, is that this is one tough world. And you ain't a tough enough kid to go around lost in it like you are."

Chapter 3

$Bu\,T$ she wasn't lost, that was the whole thing.

And as for the world — never had it been so exciting. She would sprawl out comfortably in a lounge chair on the back porch, a Coke or Pepsi and a bag of chips on the floor beside her, a book propped against her knees, and disappear into Camelot.

Or Logres or Lyonesse, Avalon or Tintagel. Into any or all of the golden kingdoms whose very names seemed made out of sun and music and summer clouds.

"A kind of tripping." Charlotte sniffed disapprovingly. "That's all it is."

"Better than pot, Char," she teased.

"Same thing if you ask me."

"Not really." Vanessa looked at her straight-faced. "Maybe if it's the same, though, I should get some. Some kids that hang around the library, they sell joints. Should I get a few?"

"You do, Baby," Charlotte snapped, "I put the biggest lump on your head you ever saw."

Vanessa laughed. "I was just kidding. But you know what we could do? I could read to you and then we could go off to Camelot together."

"I've been there."

"What do you mean, you've been there?"

"I saw the show. It was a musical."

"Where?"

"In New York. It was when I was living with my sister — you remember Dellie, she was here a couple years ago."

"Of course I remember Dellie, but . . . I didn't know there was a play about Camelot."

" 'If ever I would leave you,' " Charlotte sang, " 'it wouldn't be in summer —' You know that one."

" 'Seeing you in summer, I never would go,' " quavered Vanessa who really couldn't carry much of a tune. "— I know. Except I didn't know there was a play about Camelot. Char — who played Guinevere?"

"Julie Andrews."

"Who was Lancelot?"

"The handsome guy — we've seen him on television — what's his name? Robert Goulet, yeah, that's who it was."

"And Arthur?"

"Richard Burton."

"I know! Elizabeth Taylor."

"They're not married now."

"Oh, I wish I'd have seen it."

"It was a movie too. Maybe they'll do it on TV one of these days."

Vanessa smiled dreamily. "Anyway, Char, you know what it's like then. I mean what I'm reading and why I like it so much. It's kind of crazy in a way." She thought about it a moment. "I mean — like sometimes after I've been reading for a while I put the book down. And I look around and I can almost imagine that, well, like Camelot is all around me. I mean, like the backyards and the grass are fields, and the trees and lilac bushes are forests, and the refineries are castles. And everything — the streets and houses and people — they're all Camelot. It stretches all the way to The Bottoms."

24

Charlotte scowled. "What do you know about The Bottoms?" she demanded sharply.

"Nothing."

"You don't ever hang around there."

"No. Gram said I shouldn't."

"Well don't you ever! And you remember that!"

"I won't. I never do." She didn't tell Charlotte it was the one place in the neighborhood she was afraid of.

"Some bad things have happened to kids around there. You know that, don't you?"

"I know. I only said that Camelot goes to the edge of The Bottoms. I don't go there."

"All right then," Charlotte growled. "See that you don't. You can play your little game all you want, but you play it right here."

"Yes ma'am."

"And don't call me ma'am! It sounds too close to mammy. And I ain't your big black mammy."

Vanessa grinned. "You," she said, "are my beautiful black queen from distant Ethiopia. That's who you are."

The days came, the days went.

Vanessa read and daydreamed. She went to the library and borrowed the *Camelot* album and played it over and over until "No more!" Charlottte yelled at her. "Not one more time! You give it a rest now!" Which didn't matter, really, because she knew it all by heart anyway. She merely went on reading, only now it was even better because all the music sang along inside her as she read.

It *was* like a trip, though. Char had been right about that. She had a feeling sometimes when she was reading, as though she were being gathered up by some immense summertime river and carried slowly, serenely out of herself. Sometimes she even fell asleep for a while. Sometimes, too, she found herself reading a sentence over and over before its meaning clicked into place. But these were things that could happen to anybody and didn't mean anything.

One night she had a dream.

She dreamed that she was in school and that examinations were the next day. And she had not studied for them. Actually, this had never happened to her because she worried before exams and therefore studied like mad for them. But in the dream she had not studied all semester, and now everything had to be made up overnight. Only she did not know where to begin. And when she tried to read, some of the books had blank pages, and those that did have words seemed to make no sense to her. She began to cry, and Miss Maxwell said that she had better go home and study there. But it was dark when she got outside — darker than dark because the street lights were out and there were no lights in any houses or stores.

She began running then, up one street and down another, all of them strange. Then suddenly she was no longer in the city, but out in the countryside, running across fields, struggling through woods and thickets. She could feel thorns tearing her, the scrape of burrs. All at once she was at the edge of a cliff.

The Bottoms lay below her, the limbs of its towering trees tossing as though in a furious wind, reaching out to seize her.

"Vanessa," a voice said. She turned, and there was David. He was smiling in a terrible way. Something was dangling in his hand, something brown and limp. He was swinging it by the tail.

"Hello, Vanessa," David said.

The horror filling her was so great that she could not move.

"Vanessa — Baby!"

Arms were encircling her; she was being lifted, gathered up. "Charlotte," she half-cried.

"It's all right, baby. You all right, you just dreaming."

She held Charlotte tightly, the dream still with her. "Don't go away."

"I won't." Charlotte switched on the lamp next to the bed. "You just calm down now."

Presently the dream began breaking, gradually slipping away from her. Vanessa sighed. "I'm all right now, Char." Charlotte lowered her gently to the pillow.

"Was it a bad one, Vannie?"

Vanessa did not answer at once. She was looking back into the dream. After a while she said, "I'm not afraid now, Char. You can go back to bed."

"I don't mind staying, honey. I know what bad dreams are."

"No, it's over now. But leave the light on, will you?"

Charlotte plunked herself down in the big chair and hoisted her feet onto the coffee table. She looked like a pink porcupine with the curlers sticking up in her hair. Vanessa felt terrible.

"You're just staying home because of me," she said miserably.

Charlotte yawned. "I'm staying home 'cause I didn't want to go out with Earl. That's why I'm staying home."

"That's not true. You like Earl."

"Sure I like Earl, but he's just a dude. A big, flashy dude, nothing behind him, nothing ahead. No future with old Earl."

"You're staying home because you think something's wrong with me."

Charlotte looked at her. "Well?"

"I just haven't slept so good lately, that's all."

"So good? You ain't slept hardly at all. How many nights now you had that dream?"

"Only two."

"Same dream, though."

Vanessa nodded.

"That ain't right."

"I know it's not right, but I can't help it. I fall asleep, and then the dream comes, and after that I'm afraid to go back to sleep."

"Well, we going to put a stop to that — as of tonight. You going to sleep in my room, the other bed. You wake up, you ain't going to be there alone in the dark. I be right by you. Okay?"

"If you don't mind."

"Won't bother me none. Another thing, though, Baby — and this you got to promise me. No more reading for a while. No more daydreaming like you been doing. That's got to stop 'cause that's what's got you all upset."

"I know."

"You got to promise me that."

"I promise. I really do. I don't want to dream like this again. Ever."

"Ever" lasted two whole days.

It might have lasted longer if she hadn't felt so safe at night in the room with Charlotte. The dream had stopped. It probably wouldn't come anymore even if she did start reading. And so she did.

But the dream came that night. And the next night too.

She knew then what she had to do. It was like everything else. As long as you ran from something, it followed you. The only way you could save yourself was to face it, let it do what it had to do to you. And then try to go on from there.

The next afternoon on her way back from the library, she walked over to Front Street and along the sidewalk that skirted the edge of The Bottoms. Then, summoning up her courage, she stopped and stood there. And waited. For what, she did not really know.

Everything below her was trees, a solid green ocean of stirring leaves. To her left were the blast furnace yards, and the black smoke mixed with red flames billowing up from the stacks. From a lofty steel tower to her right, high-voltage lines swung down over The Bottoms, across the river, and up to another steel tower on the opposite side. Through a gap in the trees she could see the diked walls of the pit. The world was still as sunlight, with no motion anywhere except for the turning leaves and the smoke drifting out across the river.

Then there was another motion.

A small dark bird swept up from The Bottoms and into the smoke.

Its flight was beautiful. Then all at once frightening. There was something of the dream in it. The limbs of the trees seemed to be reaching up, clutching at the bird; it seemed to be trapped between the limbs, the coiling smoke from the stack and the high-voltage lines like a sky-hung net. She could feel the bird struggling to break free. She could feel the beat of the wings in her throat like a swelling cry.

Then it was free.

The bird banked out over the river, returned. Don't come back, she whispered. Don't. Don't. But it came, swinging wide. The sky seemed to be pulling it one way, the smoke and trees and wires another. The bird swept through the net of wires. Seemed to brush ever so slightly against a line.

Then fell, tumbling end over end. It tried to fly, but only one wing was beating. The beating wing dragged it crazily over The Bottoms.

It plunged somewhere into the diked pit.

It was as though, in some way, *she* had fallen. Fear swept over her, almost stopping her breath. She could not, dared not —

And yet . . .

She hesitated for an instant — but no longer. Marking the place in the pit where the bird had disappeared, she lunged down the ridge into The Bottoms.

Somewhere among the trees she found a path. She followed it, pushing through overhanging branches and tangles of brush and vine. Cobwebs clotted her cheeks; her dress tore at the shoulder. The woods was a vast green darkness lit only by occasional slants of sunlight. She was frightened; she had a feeling she could become even more frightened, but there was no time for that now.

Suddenly she was out of the woods and into an open field of shoulder-high yellow clover and Queen Anne's lace. The slanting wall of the pit rose ahead of her; she fought her way toward it through grass and weeds. She did not stop at the base of the wall to wonder if she could climb it, or worry about what might lie on the other side. She clawed her way upward on hands and knees, skinning herself on sharp rocks and gravel. She reached the top and would have stood up. But dared not because of the dizzying view.

She was looking down into a vast, stretching plain of sun-cracked mud enclosed on all four sides by the mountainous walls of the dike. There were two small lakes in the plain. There were marshes and sandbars. Beyond the farthest wall of the dike lay the river, and far down the river she could make out the hazy line of the horizon where the bay touched the sky. There was nothing about her but space and sky and water; nothing below but the silent continent of the plain. She crouched on the dike, the wind loosening her hair. Over one of the lakes a gull circled slowly.

She remembered the fallen bird. She stood up carefully, willing herself not to think of the space below her.

Somewhere down there . . .

Fearfully, sliding and sometimes falling, she made her way down the slope of the dike to the dried-mud shore of the pit. She scrambled along the shore to a dead, fallen tree. She stood by the tree, looking out across the pit for movement of some kind, a fluttering.

She did not hear the crack of the branches at first. The sound was part of all the sounds around her: calling birds, the moving wind, her own heart beating.

And then.it was different from these.

She turned quickly.

And there he stood. David. Staring at her.

"You," David said. He came toward her. Slowly. Terror had frozen her; she could not move. Suddenly he lunged, and the swiftness of the motion released something in her.

She was fleeing. Back along the shore. Tripping, almost falling over stone and rough clods of earth. She saw it was smoother out on the mud plain and started toward it. Heard him shouting behind her, heard the shouts growing louder, the pound of feet gaining on her.

She was struck from behind, whirled and flung to one side. She fell, rolled over and lay staring up at him. He stood over her, breathing hard, his face terrible.

He bent, lifted a rock in both hands. She covered her face.

31

"Look!" he commanded.

She looked. He hurled the rock out onto the dried mud. It broke through the crust.

Slowly, as she watched, it began sinking.

Presently it was gone.

Chapter 4

VANESSA stared at the place where the stone had disappeared.

"That's what would have happened to you."

The voice came from far away; for a moment she was not even certain she had heard a voice. She turned her head slowly in the direction from which it had come. Nothing seemed real.

David was sitting on a boulder, hunched forward, looking down at the ground between his knees. He was very pale. He seemed to be watching the sweat that dripped from the end of his nose and the point of his chin. He too was far away.

He looked at her. "What are you doing here?"

"The bird," she replied unsteadily.

"What bird?"

"The bird that fell."

"What are you talking about?"

"I was up on the ridge." She tried to keep her voice from shaking. "The bird was flying. It hit one of the wires and fell. Its one wing was hurt."

"Where did it fall?"

"Out there."

"*Where* out there?"

"I don't know. That's why I came down here, to find out."

David stood up. He was wearing a striped polo shirt and shorts made from blue jeans cropped above the knees. In school he had always seemed big to her; now, he was merely skinny. With his long hippie hair, he looked like a scarecrow nailed together out of scraps of wood. He strode away without glancing at her.

"Wait" she called out, suddenly more terrified of being alone in The Bottoms than being with him. Scrambling to her feet, she followed him along the dike, down the slope of the wall, across an open field.

Where the field ended and the woods began she saw a tent. It was a green tent, almost the color of the leaves around it, and it looked like a small house. Its roof was suspended from a rope lashed between two trees and came down almost to the ground like the letter "A." Low canvas sides ran from the roof edge to the ground. Both roof and sides were neatly and firmly staked in the ground. The entrance to the tent was hung with netting. David swept the netting aside and went in.

Vanessa halted at the entrance. Inside was an army cot with a rolled-up sleeping bag and, beside it, a collapsible canvas chair. There was an orange crate filled with pans and dishes, and two crates, one on top of the other, filled with books. There was a card table piled with boxes and wires and miscellaneous tools. There was a large packing crate on its side which, she saw, was a kind of desk because there were pencils on it and loose-leaf notebooks and an old-fashioned kerosene lamp. The tent was large enough for David to stand erect in. He lifted a pair of binoculars from a covered box and slipped them over his head. Then he seemed to notice her for the first time.

34

"What are you hanging around here for?" he demanded roughly.

She did not know what to say.

He came through the tent flap, deliberately shouldering her aside, and hurried across the field. She waited until he had climbed to the top of the dike, then followed him. She crouched low on the dike and watched.

He moved away from her along the dike, stopping from time to time to scan the pit with his glasses. Soon he was at the far end of the pit, a tiny figure walking a narrow dirt wall between the sky and the lake in the pit below. He turned and walked toward the river, then came back to that part of the wall running along the river. She watched him come toward her.

"Are you sure you saw a bird?" he said.

"Yes."

"I looked. I covered every inch of ground with my glasses. There's nothing."

"I saw it fall."

"You didn't see anything." He stared at her coldly. "You imagined it."

"I didn't! I saw it!"

"Are you calling me a liar?"

"No, but —"

"You're calling me a liar, that's what you're doing. Now listen to me!" He jerked his hand in the direction of the woods. "You get out of here and you get fast."

She stared at him dumbly.

"I haven't forgotten what you did to me in school. And what I promised you. You come down here once more — I ever catch you again — you're going to get it, the full treatment. Now beat it!"

She could not move. Or speak. Words were tumbling

around inside her head but she could not catch hold of them.

"Didn't you hear what I said?" His voice rose threateningly. "Get going."

She began to whimper.

Because at that moment she did not really know where she was, or how to find her way back.

"Stop that!" he ordered.

"I can't go through those woods."

"You don't have to, stupid." He pointed toward a utility pole far across the field to the left. "See that pole over there? Just beyond it is a path. It'll take you up to the ridge so you won't have to go through the woods." He gave her a shove. "Now move it — and don't ever come down here again."

But he could not keep her away.

She came back that night while he tossed about on his cot, trying to sleep. Although it was not her at first.

It was the thought of the bird somewhere out in the pit — if there was a bird.

Alive and in pain.

He had seen nothing when he looked. He had been very careful, almost a hundred percent sure there was nothing — but he could not be completely sure. The bird could be there, somewhere among the stones or in the marsh grass. Alive in its pain and no one knowing.

Like the herring gull with the broken wing he had found on the shore that day near Gloucester. He should have tried to set the wing, but he hadn't because he was afraid of causing the gull more pain. And he could not kill it either. So he had walked away. He had left the gull there on the bleak granite shelf, the wind flapping the torn wing, and walked away. As he had walked away from other hurt

36

things — because he could neither bear to hurt them further, nor nerve himself to the merciful act of ending their hurt.

Which was the kind of freak he was.

So even if there had been a bird this afternoon, and he *had* found it, would he have been able to —?

He pushed the question from his mind. Which didn't work because immediately, into the place where it had been, swept that other and darker question he had been tormenting himself with lately.

Who are you anyway?

It was an unsettling question because on the surface there was no sense to it. He knew who he was, and there was nothing confusing or complicated about it. He was himself, just as all the other people he knew were themselves. It was a thing there could be no question about. Yet for him the question remained.

For it seemed to him that there were two David Pinkhams.

There was David the First who was cool and self-reliant, who could go his way alone and didn't need friends. Who could swim and sail a dinghy and climb mountains and live off the land — all of which he had proved over the years in endless summer camps. There was this David whom he liked and was proud of being.

Then there was the other, David the Second. Who was a coward. Who was afraid of pain. Who, for all his swimming, was afraid of water; for all his climbing, afraid of heights. Who was afraid of the pit where he was camped, and the treacherous mud floor of the pit, which could at any time break through. And no matter what the other David did, or even proved, this one was always slouching around in the background muttering, "I'm still here and I'm what you are and you haven't proved anything."

And no reason for any of it — that was the thing. He had brought reason to bear on all his fears, used reason to fight them. But reason never worked. It was imagination, his father said; he had too much of it. And maybe it was. Still, that didn't solve anything. He was still afraid. And because he was, somehow — in everything, it seemed — he had a way of always defeating himself.

Maybe that was what was wrong with him — why he was always behind everyone else in school and not particularly good at anything. Maybe all he was good for was living alone in a tent and watching birds and keeping records on them. And even with this he hadn't been so good today, because it wasn't he who had seen the bird fall, but the girl.

And with that thought, she was suddenly there in the tent. And like all the other things he had turned his back on — hurting him. He had to go on thinking about her then. There was no escape.

He remembered her standing there in the pit, the look on her face when she had turned and seen him. It was like the day he had laid the dead mouse in her hand. The same look. The same leap of fear. As though something had splintered inside her, like glass, but hadn't broken. But a breath of air, or the slightest touch of anything, could make fall apart. That was the look.

And the thing was, he understood it.

It was the look he sensed in his own eyes sometimes. He had experienced the same crazy sensation of cracked glass.

That was what bothered him, what kept hurting in a way. She might be like him, only he had never stopped to think of it. The way he remembered her in school, she had always looked scrubbed, her hair just freshly washed. One of the clean, precious mama's darlings he had always

38

despised, one of the smart kids in every class who made him look dumb. And yet maybe all that was just front, the same kind of front he was putting up all the time. Maybe under it was the fear, the little cracked pieces of glass just holding together. Maybe she was as screwed up in her way as he was in his. Damaged, like the gull, and separated from the rest of the birds by its damage. Only you couldn't see it.

But it was there.

He awakened sometime during the night to find himself crying. It was startling, yet not too startling either, because he had been dreaming about the gull which, in the dream, was lost somewhere down in the pit. In a deeper way, though, it wasn't the gull he was crying about, but the girl, Vanessa.

She was lost in another kind of pit. And like all the birds and animals he had tried to help, and from whom he had fled because he could not help, she was making an impossible claim on him.

Chapter 5

CHARLOTTE watched from behind the screen door.

Each time the boy had walked past, he had sneaked a furtive look at the house. Then he had crossed the street, walked back on the other side, sneaking his look again, and gone on. Three times around like this and now on his way back again. Charlotte opened the screen door, went down the porch steps and out to the sidewalk. She waited at the end of the walk, hoping he'd get smart and start sassing her. Ready for him. She watched him approach, head lowered, a tall, skinny kid in shorts with a mean face and too much hair. He would have walked past.

"You," she said.

He stopped short. "Yes, ma'am?"

"You looking for somebody?"

"No, ma'am."

"What you doing around here?"

"Just walking."

"I been watching you walking. Each time you come past here you look in. Who you looking for?"

"Nobody."

"Your name David?"

"Yes, ma'am."

"You looking for Vanessa, ain't you?"

He swallowed and thought about it. "Yes, ma'am."

"Why you lie about it then?"

He shook his head. "I don't know."

She looked at him sternly. "You the boy who put that dead mouse in her hand, ain't you?" He nodded. "You the one who's been laying for her too, ain't you? That's what you doing here now, laying for her."

"No."

"That's another lie."

"No, ma'am, it isn't."

"Then what you hanging 'round here for?"

He looked down at the sidewalk and scuffed around at it with his toe. Something in her relented a little. The boy's face was not mean, only troubled. The trouble made it look mean. "Listen," she said, "I'm going to tell you something. That little girl, she's scared to death of you, what you say you're going to do to her. Maybe you don't mean it. Maybe you just trying to scare her. And if that's the case, you done it all right. Bad."

His face was pained. "I kind of figured that."

"You figured that?" She was surprised, then immediately angry. "Then what you doing it for? You coming 'round now to torment her again?"

"No, ma'am. Honest I'm not."

"Then why you here?"

"I thought maybe — if she was around she could — I mean I'd ask her if she wanted to — you know, come down and . . ."

"Come down where? What you talking about?"

"The other day, what happened. I didn't mean — you know . . ."

"I don't know nothing. What you trying to say?"

"Didn't she tell you?"

"About what?"

"The other day. The bird, the one she saw fall."

"She didn't tell me nothing about no bird."

David told her. Not very well, not without shame, but at least honestly. Not sparing himself. ". . . that's why I came by," he added. "I thought maybe if I saw her around I'd try to . . ." He shrugged helplessly, not quite knowing how to finish it.

"You telling me the truth?" Charlotte said.

He met her gaze squarely. "Yes, ma'am."

She studied him. "I believe you," she said finally. "I don't know why I should, but I believe you. You could maybe even help her — if you really want to — 'cause she's plenty upset, and you're behind most of it. You want to talk to her?"

"May I?"

"She's in the backyard. You can go back." She scowled. "You listen, though. You try to do anything to her, you going to be in deep trouble."

"I'm not going to do anything. I promise."

"You see you keep it, that's all."

"May I go back now?"

"Yeah. Go ahead."

David walked around the side of the house to a picket gate. He unlatched the gate — and stopped. Vanessa was sitting on the back porch steps. There was an open book in her lap but she was not reading it. She was staring out at something — or nothing — in the yard. He closed the gate and waited for her to turn around. When she did not, he approached her hesitantly.

"Hi," he ventured.

She turned her head and looked at him.

She looked through him as though he weren't there. Her face was the tight, frozen face he remembered from school. Not a feature moved.

Then the lips moved. "What do you want?"

42

"I was talking to your friend, the black lady. She said I could come back." He lowered himself cautiously to the bottom step. It was as though she were some small frightened creature hiding behind her face; his instinct for creatures went out to her. "I told her about the other day," he said carefully. "How you saw the bird and we looked for it."

The face merely stared.

"I didn't have the chance to tell you, but I was glad you saw it and told me. Even though we didn't find it." He groped about for words. "Do you like birds?"

She could have been a statue.

"I mean, do you know anything about them?" He waited for a reply. "I could teach you if you'd like to know."

The statue stared at him.

"Listen," he said abruptly. "There's something I've got to say." He decided it would be better not to look at her. "About what happened in school, the mouse and everything. I'm sorry. I didn't mean to — No, I guess I did mean to at the time. I thought it would be fun or something. But it wasn't. I felt kind of stinking about it as a matter of fact. I didn't want to go on scaring you the way I did either, but somehow I . . ." He shook his head. "I'm kind of screwed up in a lot of ways, I guess. That's what my father says anyway, and he's probably right. The thing is, though, I'm sorry. I mean it. It won't happen again." He drew a long breath. "That's a promise."

There was silence then. Only the leaves of the trees stirring, and the voices of kids playing in the alley, and the occasional slam of a screen door. Somewhere down on the river a tugboat hooted. He sneaked a glance at her.

She was crying. She was making no sound and her face was without expression. The tears simply ran out of her eyes and down her cheeks.

43

"Don't," he said.

The crying went on.

"I told you I'm sorry. I really am."

But it was no use. He got to his feet and hurried from the yard. Charlotte was on the front porch. "Well?" she said.

"She's crying," he said unhappily. "I didn't do anything to her."

"I know. I was watching."

"I told her I was sorry. I tried to be friends."

"And she wouldn't have it."

"She didn't say anything, she just looked at me. Then she started to cry."

Charlotte looked at him long and thoughtfully. "Let me ask you a question," she said. "You say you want to be friends with her. You really want to be?"

He glanced at her, puzzled.

"That ain't exactly a dumb question. 'Cause I'm going to tell you something. You don't have to be friends with her if you don't want. You came up here, and you said you was sorry, and you tried to be nice. You tried, and it ain't your fault it didn't work out. So you can go now and no need to feel bad about anything. You don't owe her nothing. On the other hand, maybe you want to be friends. I don't know, that's up to you. All I'm saying is, you don't have to be if you don't want. So what you want to do?"

He thought about it, although, in a way, there was nothing to think about. He really didn't want to be friends; he didn't want her hanging around the pit and bothering him. And he *had* tried, he *had* said he was sorry. He had even meant it about teaching her about birds. He had done all he could do and it wasn't his fault that it hadn't worked out.

"You can walk away from here now," Charlotte said,

44

"and you don't need to feel bad about nothing. You been a good boy for trying . . ."

But then that's what he had always done, hadn't he? With the gull, with the bird in the pit, with all the other hurt things he had left behind him. The same thing he wanted to do now with the girl back there on the porch, more hurt than any of them.

". . . on the other hand, you want to try it again I'll see what I can do. I ain't making no promises though."

And all at once there was nothing more to think about.

"I'd like to try it," he said.

"Okay then, you run along. Maybe today yet, maybe tomorrow. I'll talk to her, see if I can work something out."

Chapter 6

*T*H*AT* night Charlotte said, "I didn't much like him either. At first. But after I talked to him for a while I sort of changed my mind."

Charlotte said, "After all, he didn't have to come around and apologize. But he did. You got to give him credit for that."

She said, "Baby, you going to think I'm crazy for saying this, but — Whyn't you go down to that place of his, see what it's like. It might be fun. For both of you."

Finally, "Matter of fact, I think you *should* go down there and give it a try."

Vanessa said in a small voice, "Even though it's The Bottoms?"

Charlotte nodded. "Will you go?"

"Yes."

What else was there to say?

She couldn't, of course. It was impossible. She would have to find some way of getting out of it. She lay awake, long after Charlotte had fallen asleep, trying to think of a way. But there was none. If it were any day but tomorrow she could lie her way out of it. Charlotte would be at work, she wouldn't know, she would believe her if she said she went down to the pit. But tomorrow was Sunday. There was no way out.

Unless it was raining.

Unless she was sick.

But in the morning neither had happened.

"After lunch," Charlotte said, "I'll walk you down there. I want to see this bird place myself."

All the way down, it was like a dream. The worst kind. Worse even than the real one that had started all the trouble. And no way out. None. She was scarcely conscious of the path down through the trees, the open field, climbing the wall of the dike.

All at once she became aware of voices.

". . . five o-clock."

"Yes, ma'am."

Of the wind blowing. Of sun. Of dazzling space.

". . . that don't mean half past five, it don't even mean ten past. It mean five. If she ain't back to the house by that time, I be down here after her and, for you, that won't be the least little bit good."

And then she was alone on top of the dike.

And David looking at her worriedly, seeming not to know what to do next.

"Well . . ." he said.

For the first time, the thought struck her: Maybe this is as bad for him as it is for me. And with the thought, something steadied in her.

"What would you like to do?" he asked.

"I don't know. What would you like to do?"

He raised the binoculars that were around his neck and looked down into the pit. They seemed to be pointed at the shore of one of the lakes. They moved slowly along the shore.

"What are you looking for?" she asked timidly.

"You."

She stared at him.

"You're down there. Somewhere. I saw you yesterday."

"You're crazy," she said simply.

"Matter of fact, I saw three of you." He lowered the glasses and looked at her. Then he nodded his head solemnly. "*Calidris alpina*," he said. Suddenly he grinned, a wide, pumpkin grin full of crooked and comic teeth. "Dunlins," he said. "Haven't you ever heard of dunlins?"

"That's my name," she said foolishly.

"Your name and theirs. *Calidris alpina* is their Latin name. Hey, let's sit down and give ourselves a lower profile." Vanessa lowered herself obediently into the high grass on top of the dike. "It's always a good idea to sit low when you're bird watching, blend into the landscape as much as you can."

"What are dunlins?" Vanessa asked.

"Shorebirds. A species of sandpiper. They have a kind of reddish back and fairly long bills. But the way you tell them this time of year, they have a dark spot on the breast. You can't miss it."

"Do they live around here?"

"You don't know anything about birds, do you?"

"No."

"You're going to have to learn if you want to be any help down here."

"Help?"

"Sure. That's what I told your friend. I told her you could maybe be of some help to me, and it might be fun for you too."

"What would I have to do?"

"Well — look around you. See the woods back there, the one you came through? Woods like that are a special kind of bird habitat — like only certain kinds of birds live in woods. Then you've got the open fields — that's another

48

kind of habitat with its own kinds of birds. Okay, now you look down there into the pit and you've got two lakes, their shorelines, some marshes. So right here in this little area around us, you could say there are at least three distinct bird habitats."

Vanessa was mystified — yet, in spite of herself, interested. "So?" she said.

"So this. I've got a project going here. Sort of, you know, like our science projects in school. Only this one's my own. Okay, you say, what's the project?" He pointed out across the pit. "All along the river here is one of the most polluted areas in the state. On account of the refineries and blast furnaces and factories. Both air and water pollution. The University ran an environmental study of it last year and that's what they found. So what I'm doing is, I'm running a bird study. I want to find out what effect this kind of pollution has on birds. Like, I mean, do they still come here? And if they do, what species come and what species nest? And what do they feed on, and what happens during the migration season? Things like that."

"But what could *I* do?"

"Like I say, it's a big area. There's a lot of ground to cover. And I keep records on everything. What you could do is help me keep them. 'Course, you'd have to learn to recognize birds and keep counts on them, but I could teach you that."

Vanessa felt dizzy. Everything was happening so fast, it was confusing.

"You don't have to make up your mind now or anything. You can think about it. The main thing is, I guess, would you like to?"

She did not know.

But the question had been asked.

It seemed to be hanging in the air between them. But how could she give an answer when so many things were swinging around in her head?

"I — I don't know," she finally said. And then, because that did not seem to be enough — and she did not know what else to say — she said the first thing that came into her mind. "Do you live down there in the tent? All the time?"

Which she knew was stupid as soon as she said it. But he didn't seem to mind.

"Most of the time."

"Just by yourself?"

"What's wrong with that?"

"Nothing. Except isn't it kind of — you know — I mean, lonely?"

"No."

"Doesn't your father care?"

"He thinks my project is a good one. It also keeps me out of trouble, he says."

"Don't you ever see him?"

"Oh, sure. I go home on Saturday afternoons and we go shopping, and I get stocked up with food and stuff for a week. We usually spend Saturday and Sunday together — except today. He had to work."

Vanessa shook her head. "I guess I don't understand."

"About what?"

"You. Living like this. Your father — I mean, not seeing much of each other. I don't know, it's just . . ." She gestured helplessly.

David smiled. "Hard to understand."

She nodded.

"Well, it's like this," he said. "My father, he's an engineer, a petroleum engineer. Sort of a troubleshooter. He travels around to refineries where they have problems and helps clear them up. And I go with him. You see, my mother died two years ago and there's just the two of us. So I have to go with him — except that I'd want to anyway."

"Don't you have any brothers or sisters?"

"Not that I could live with. My one brother, Tom, is with the Peace Corps. And my oldest brother, Everett, he's working on his Ph.D at Columbia. So we don't see too much of each other anymore. No, it's my father and me now, but we're a pretty good team together."

"But you just go drifting around the country."

"We don't drift." David's voice was a little sharp. "We're on assignment. There's a big difference. Anyway, though, that's the way we live. Say, for example, my father gets an assignment somewhere. We pack up and go there. Then we look for an apartment in a nice part of town near a good school — that's a big thing with my father, the school bit — and then we settle in. Sometimes it's only for a few months, but most of the time it's for a year or longer."

"Then why," Vanessa asked, "are you living here?" She saw David's puzzled expression. "I mean this is *not* a nice part of town. And it's probably not the greatest school in the world either."

"It just sort of happened, I guess. Like when we first came, we didn't expect to be here very long. Not even a month, my father thought. It didn't look like one of the big projects. So there didn't seem much point in going through the usual apartment-hunting bit. We just took a few rooms in this place near the refinery — it's a kind of big rooming house on Front Street."

"Is it Mrs. Salter's?"

"How did you know?"

"I just guessed. My grandmother has told me about her. Her husband used to work at the refinery and they say she only rents to refinery people."

"Well, that's where we are. Anyway, what happened is that the job turned out to be bigger than my father thought, so we had to stay on. Then pretty soon it was time for school to start and — I guess it was easier to stay where we were than go on a crash hunt for some other place. Although from what my father says, we probably won't be here much longer."

"Where will you go then?"

"Wherever we're assigned. Back to Pennsylvania, maybe. Or Texas again, or California. I don't know. My father would like to go home again. I would too."

"Where is home?"

"In Massachusetts. Wellfleet. It's on the Cape. We haven't been back there for a long while." He was silent a moment. "Not since my mother died."

Vanessa looked at him. Something seemed different about him, almost looked different — although what it was she was not exactly certain. Or maybe it was that she had never really looked at him before.

She took a deep breath. "Do you . . . I mean, do you really want me to come down here . . . and teach me about birds or . . . like are you trying to make up for . . . things?"

He thought about it, then shrugged. "Well, to be honest, when I went up to your place yesterday I guess I just wanted to make up for the lousy way I'd been treating you. I really didn't want you to come down or show you about birds. But now — it's sort of different now." He nodded. "I'd like you to come. I really would. If you'd like to."

Vanessa looked at him for a long moment.

52

"I'd like to," she said. The words surprised her. She swallowed hard. "When will you start teaching me?"

"Right now." He lifted the binoculars off his neck and slipped them around hers. "First thing you have to do is learn to use these. Go ahead, look through them. What do you see?"

"It's all blurry."

"All right." He pointed into the pit. "Focus on that big rock down there." He showed her how to adjust the glasses, keeping first one eye closed, then the other. "Now look through both eyes."

The rock leaped at her through the glasses and settled down so close she felt she could almost touch it. She could see the cracks in it, the individual pebbles around it. She swung the glasses to the nearby water. What had been little wind wrinkles on its surface were now magnified into small moving waves. The world was a dancing, glittering miracle. It began to shake. She lowered the glasses.

"They're probably too heavy for you," David said. "They're ten by fifty, but you'll get used to them. Let's look for a bird now. There's one — see? Try to pick it up. Use just your center focus now."

Vanessa trained the glasses, her hands trembling. She found the bird. It was beautiful, like black velvet, so close she could see the speck of sun glint in one eye.

"Got it?"

"Yes."

"What does it look like? Describe it."

"It's dark. Black almost. It's got red on its wings."

"Just red?"

"N-no, there's a little yellow above the red." She had to lower the glasses. "What is it?"

He shook his head. "I could tell you, but that wouldn't

do you any good. You've got to learn to track it down by yourself. And the way you do that is the way all bird people do." He reached into his hip pocket and handed her a book. "Old Roger Tory Peterson."

She opened the book and riffled through its pages. Birds by the tens, the hundreds soared up from its pages. So many, so varied, her head spun.

"I'll never find it in here," she said despairingly.

"Yes you will. Once you know how. I'll tell you the secret." He scrunched himself over beside her, took the book and closed it. "The way this book is arranged," he said, "it begins with sea birds, like gulls. Then ducks, which can be either sea birds or lake birds. Then come the marsh birds. Then birds of the shore, like the dunlins, your name. Then large land birds, then smaller and smaller land birds until at the end you come to the sparrows. The thing to remember is, you start with the sea and gradually work your way to shore and then to the land."

"I can't remember that."

"Of course you can't, not at first. Nobody can. But I'll show you how to go about it. Take the book now and pay attention. That bird out there, you wouldn't call it a sea bird, would you?"

"No."

"So all right. When you start looking in the book — go ahead now — you won't waste your time on the sea birds."

She began turning the color plates in the book.

"It's not a duck either, is it?"

"No."

She turned past the ducks. Then the herons and galli-nules. She turned pages of hawks, owls, woodpeckers, hummingbirds.

"Go slow now," David said. "Look carefully."

She turned past the jays and starlings.

"Hold it!"

Vanessa looked at him.

"Don't look at me. Look at the page there."

She looked down at the page, but could not find the bird. Then she found it.

"A redwing blackbird?" she asked excitedly.

David nodded.

"It's here! I actually found it!"

David handed her a pencil and a small pad. "Write it down. The name of the bird and where you saw it. Just write: The pit. Marsh edge near Lake #1. Then the date, June 16. That'll do for now."

"Is this what you do with every bird?"

"I don't. But you do because you're a beginner, and this is the way you learn. You keep a list."

Vanessa looked at what she had written, then down into the pit and across the lake to the far wall of the dike. She looked at the book in her lap. Then at David.

"What should I do now?" she asked happily.

"Start building your list."

Chapter 7

*I*T seemed to have happened overnight.

Camelot was gone.

Not lost, because it was a part of her and would always be so. She had lived in it for a short while, and so intensely that she knew it would continue to be with her, as real in its way as Gram and Charlotte were real. But she would never try to return to it.

There was another reality now.

It was all around her; it didn't have to be read or dreamed. It was a thing she could live in and trust.

Although there did seem an impossible lot to learn.

"Where did you see it?" David demanded.

"Down there in the reeds." Vanessa handed him the glasses. He trained them on the bird.

"I've got news for you," he said. "That's no short-billed marsh wren."

"It is so."

"No way."

"I checked it in the book."

"You checked wrong." He handed the glasses back, "Look again. See the white line over the eye, the black and white stripes on the back? The solid crown, no streaking? That's a long-billed, my friend."

"Hmmm."

"It's an easy mistake to make, but you wouldn't have made it if you'd been more careful."

"All right, so I goofed," she grumbled.

"You've been goofing all day, you know that?"

"I have not."

"You fouled up on those peeps this morning, calling them 'leasts' when they were semipalmated. You should have known from the dark legs what they were. And that black-crowned night heron — you called it a yellow-crowned. And that robin — Good Lord, if you'd have taken the trouble to look at it, you'd have seen it was a Baltimore oriole."

He sounded impatient with her, even a little cross. Her face grew hot.

"Any more days like this, Dunlin, I'm flunking you out of the course."

She looked at him, stunned. And saw at once the tease in his eyes and the pumpkin-wide grin. And felt suddenly foolish. "David, sometimes I could . . ."

"Could what?"

"I don't know."

"You believed that? About flunking you?"

"How was I to know? You sounded so crabby."

"I thought you were getting on to my weird sense of humor."

"I am. Only sometimes . . ."

"Look, Vanessa, I've been on bird hikes with adults, guys who have been in the field fifteen, twenty years. And I've seen them pull just as dumb things as you did. Everybody does. Me?" He shook his head. "Last summer I pegged a scarlet tanager a cardinal, and you can't get any worse than that."

* * *

". . . but the truth is I was pretty bad," Vanessa said. "David says it's because I'm trying too hard to add to my list."

"He does, does he?" Charlotte remarked.

Vanessa nodded. "It's probably true. David said — "

"David said this, David said that. Everything is David these days."

Vanessa felt uncomfortable. "Well, you know," she said lamely.

"Do I only know!"

"Know what?"

Charlotte took a pink curler out of her mouth, worked it into her hair and began rolling it. "You eleven now, going on twelve. You getting that old feeling."

"I don't know what you're talking about, Char," she said primly.

"Oh yes you do, Baby. And they ain't nothing wrong with it either. I'm all for it. But you got it."

"We're just friends, Char. We have fun together."

"You kinda like him a little bit, though, don't you?"

Vanessa thought about it. And all at once saw something — something that had been there for some time without her being aware of it. She tried to conceal it, as much from herself as from Charlotte. "He's all right, I guess," she said with affected carelessness — knowing even as she said it that she wasn't fooling anyone.

Everything was all right.

Everything, Vanessa thought solemnly, right now, is more wonderful than anything in my whole life.

Even the smallest things, like the way time passed and the days went by.

It wasn't something you kept track of by the hands on your watch, or separated into sevens like days of the week.

It was a new kind of time, a stately flowing of days merging one into another. David felt it too and said it was like the ocean in a way: the tides going out and coming in, but the ocean always the same. And yet every tide and every new day brought its changes.

At first the woods were filled with warblers, the thickets with song sparrows and goldfinches. Meadowlarks, redwings and grackles swept and crisscrossed the open fields. One day over the pit a pair of black terns appeared, ghostly as twin dark moths. One day a kingfisher, tearing her breath away with the slash of its blue and rust body, plunged into the river and immediately rose, a small, silvery fish in its beak. In the mornings, herons flapped over the lakes in the pit and mallards cruised on their surface like tiny flotillas of ships. Toward dusk, nighthawks circled and dived open-beaked through the insect swarms rising from the marshes.

There was change of this kind; then gradually there came change of another.

The herons disappeared. Mallards and teals rose from the lakes and did not return. One day the terns were gone, one day the yellowlegs and the white, heavenly egrets. The lakes cleared of bird life and grew still. One afternoon, toward dusk, hundreds of sandpipers rose from the sand flats of the pit, filling the dark, amethyst air with their haunting peeps and twitterings and did not return.

Something is happening, Vanessa thought. She said nothing to David, partly because she didn't know what it was, but mostly because David, whom nothing escaped, seemed unaware of anything wrong. But something *was* wrong. The birds were leaving. Not just birds anymore, but her birds, those that were closest and dearest to her because they were the first whose names she had learned, and whose forms and patterns of flight had entered into her. Now they were going, and the emptying sky and the emptiness filling the pit was one with the emptiness gathering inside her. It hurt. A kind of vast hurt seemed to lie over everything in the pit.

"Why?" she cried to David when she could bear it no longer. "Why is it happening?"

He looked at her curiously. "What?"

"The birds, the way they've been leaving?"

"Migration," he said. "I should have told you. They're on their way to the breeding grounds. Most of them anyway. It's normal, the way it should be. In fact, those around here are late. The big wave went through here a few weeks ago. The dull part of the season is beginning now."

"I miss them."

"They'll be back."

"When?"

"Late July, early August they'll start coming. Or I hope. they will. That's one of the things we're trying to find out — will they come back to a high-pollution area? That's one of the reasons for record-keeping. We can compare the northward migration counts with the southward and see what happens."

"But they will be back?"

"I'm pretty sure. Don't worry."

The only birds left now, it seemed, were the common ones, which had been around all the time — those she had been vaguely aware of without really noticing.

One day she fell in love with one of them, a small brown bird that seemed to roll out of the wind itself, blown like a leaf but not at all like a leaf because its motion was all its own. It swirled over the pit, a gay, mad little clown of a

60

bird, swooping and somersaulting so swiftly in pursuit of insects that she could not hold it in the binoculars. So she forgot about the glasses and merely watched, delighting in the pure antic movement of its flight. It seemed to be flying for the joy of flight, and laughing at its own tumbling tomfoolery.

And then for no reason it flew straight at the wall of the dike across from her, crashing into it.

Vanessa cried out; she could not help it. It was so sudden, so cruel: the bird broken, its joy broken, like shattered glass. She focused the binoculars on the bank, looking for the small brown body, but could not find it against the brown dike wall. She stood up. She would have to search for it now, find it and bury it. She owed it that much for the way it had caught up her heart and whirled it across the sky.

And then as suddenly as it died, it came alive. She saw it come out of the loose gravel and clay of the dike and sweep over the pit. And then plunge back into the dike. She trained the glasses on the place where it entered, found a small hole, then tiers of small holes about it. Then saw that the holes were squirming with birds going and coming. It was like watching a swarm of bees. She settled herself to watch steadily. She tried to feel herself into the tiny brown bodies and clown through the air with them, gathering insects and returning again and again to their cool, earthen burrows and the nestlings inside. She began taking notes.

"A rough-wing," David said. "Not a bad observation there."

"Are you sure?"

"Sure I'm sure."

61

"I mean," she said hesitatingly, "I don't think it is. It looks more like a bank swallow."

"Don't contradict the old master," he said with just the slightest hint of reprimand. "You know better than that."

Vanessa handed him the glasses. "Look again, David."

"I don't need to, it's a rough-wing."

"It has a breast band, though. Maybe you didn't see it."

"I don't make mistakes like that." Nevertheless, he took the glasses and focused on the bank. After a few moments he lowered them. "You're right, Vannie, absolutely right." There was a curious respect in his eyes. "I think you've come of age."

"What does that mean?"

"The course is over. You've passed. A-plus."

Vanessa laughed delightedly. "Do you mean it, David?"

He nodded. "You're ready now. For the big time."

"And what's that?"

"Well . . . like up until now, you've been sort of learning the business. I couldn't rely, you know, a hundred percent on your observations — but I can now. This swallow bit does it. So from here on, I'm going to turn you loose on your own. Your counts and your reports are going into the official record. But first" — it seemed to her that his face darkened for an instant — "I'm going to have to take you down into the pit and show you a few things."

The bottom of the pit was more frightening than she allowed herself to admit.

"You can see why I haven't let you come down here before," David said.

The two lakes seemed immense, their shorelines extending forever. Deserts of gravel and cracked-mud flats stretched between them. In the marsh areas reeds and cattails towered over her head. David pointed to a sign with bold red lettering:

WARNING

LAND FILL AREA

GROUND WILL NOT BEAR WEIGHT

KEEP OUT

U.S. ARMY CORPS OF ENGINEERS

"This sign," he said; "it's the most important thing in the pit. Keep it in mind every time you come down here. It means what it says."

"But we're down here. The ground's bearing our weight."

"That's because it's dry and because I know where to walk. I'll show you what I mean." He walked a short distance from her, stopped and stood for a moment. There was something tense, almost crouching about his body. When he turned his face she could see sweat. He is afraid, she thought. And immediately, with the thought, she could feel his fear reaching back to her.

"Stand here," he commanded.

She stood beside him.

And felt it. A deep, heavy swaying under her. A thick unsteadiness. As though she were standing on a stiff crust of Jello.

"Feel it?"

She nodded.

"This is what the sign means." He led her back to dryer, stonier ground and wiped his face with the back of his hand. "This whole damned pit is built up of layers and layers of muck they've dredged out of the river. It dries on top, but you can never be sure how deep it dries. There are

63

places you can break through. And after a rain the whole place is deadly. So you've got to be careful, you've got to test every place you walk. But there are some places you can be reasonably safe on most of the time. That's what I'm going to show you now, so pay attention. I mean but real attention."

Vanessa spent the rest of the afternoon in the pit, learning it. She learned that the shorelines around the lakes were treacherous, except where there were gravel banks. That the hard sand bars extending into the lakes were safe. She learned to look everywhere for rocks and boulders because, in general, these areas were safe. She learned where to walk and where not to walk, and David made her go over these routes until she was ready to drop. Even when, from sheer weariness, she began to cry he would not let her off, but kept coaxing and teasing in his crazy way to make her go on.

"I hate you, I could kill you," she flamed at him.

"I don't blame you. But I want you to learn this ground."

"You're cruel. You like being cruel."

"You know better than that."

And because she did, and because she hated herself when she whined, she went on stumbling along beside him.

She punished him, though: she did not speak to him. She put up a wall of silence around her and sulked inside it, enjoying in a strange, bitter way the pleasure of blocking him out. Hurting, she found, could be fun. But when David, too, stopped talking, the hurt turned against her and nothing was fun. She wanted to take away the wall but did not know how, and she had left no door in it to go through. And the terrible thing was that she knew, really knew, he was doing all this for her because he cared and

64

was afraid for her. As he was afraid for himself. It was something she knew without knowing how she knew. And she could not tell him. He was outside the wall walking alone, even as she was walking alone inside.

It might have ended that way.

All the long walk homeward David said nothing; outside the house he would have turned away without a word. And she would have, too, except that all at once she grew up.

"David?" she said in a low voice.

"Mmmmm?"

"I'm sorry."

"About what?"

"The way I acted. I didn't mean it."

"I pushed you pretty hard. I shouldn't have, maybe."

"You just wanted me to learn."

"That's all I wanted."

"You're not mad, are you?"

"No."

It was funny in a way. He looked at her, and she had a feeling he wanted to say something but didn't know how to say it. Then he shrugged his shoulders sort of helplessly and bumped his fist in a gentle way against the tip of her nose. "You're a good guy, Dunlin," he muttered. "You're okay." And lurched off, to her bewilderment, almost at a run.

And to his own bewilderment when he became aware of it.

He slowed down. Where was he going? What was the hurry? It was still only late afternoon, the whole night lay ahead. Besides, he didn't really want to go back to the pit. What he would have liked, what would have been fun, would have been to stay there on the porch with her for a while. Just talk, horse around. Nothing special. Maybe walk up Front Street to the Kone & Kream for a malted or something. She would have liked it too. But then for no reason, while he was talking with her there, everything had gotten very complicated inside him. So complicated he hadn't known how to handle it, so the only thing to do, it seemed, was to take off.

Which he hadn't wanted.

Just as what he had said, that dumb, phoney-sounding line, like something out of an old Bogie rerun on television, he hadn't wanted that either. You're a good guy, Dunlin, you're okay.

He had meant it, but it didn't cover things.

He had meant a lot more.

That was what was so confusing.

Someone was in the tent.

He knew it at once, even before he noticed the faint layer of smoke hanging above the opening. Then he smelled the smoke.

He swept aside the tent flap. "Dr. Pinkham, I presume?"

The big man grinned. His bulldog pipe seemed suspended from a corner of the grin.

David laughed. "Alice in Wonderland," he said.

"You or me?"

"Neither. The Cheshire Cat, the smile floating in the air. Only this one's got a pipe in it." He went into the tent and sagged down beside his father. "What brings you down, Dad?"

"Groceries. I though you could use some supplies."

"Can I only."

"Also some Cokes. Also one of those Styrofoam hampers and some dry ice. The Cokes are inside."

"Good man."

"I thought I might find you and your assistant down here."

"I just took her home."

"When am I going to meet her?"

"One of these days."

"I was thinking, we could go out to dinner some night, the three of us. What do you think?"

"I'd like that."

"I'll leave it up to you. Set something up and we'll do it."

"Vanessa would like it too."

"You know something? I'm kind of glad Vanessa is around, that you're not alone all the time. I worry about it."

"You shouldn't worry, I can take care of myself. You know that."

"I know. Otherwise I wouldn't have let you come down here. Still . . . maybe it's another kind of aloneness that bothers me. Ours. Yours and mine."

"What do you mean, Dad?"

"This crazy way we live. You going your way, me going mine. I know we can't help it, neither of us. It's the nature of my work — moving around, never being settled. You've had to be on your own, more or less, whether you wanted to be or not. Still, what it adds up to is that you've got a father who is never around and I have a son I don't see near enough of. I don't know what to do about it either, and it worries me."

"We'll make out, Dad. We always have."

"But you're getting older. And you're getting older very well without me. And while that's a good thing in one way, in another . . ." He patted David's knee. "Forget it. I'm feeling sorry for myself, and I'm too old — or I should be — for that kind of silliness. Let's just say that I'm glad you're not alone now, that you've got a friend to keep you company." He stood up. "Well, I suppose you'd like to get out on the dike and get to work. I'll drift on back to the house and work up a couple reports I've been putting off."

"Do you have to?"

"I should."

"I've got a better idea. Why don't we break out a couple Cokes, and then afterward you come out on the dike with me?"

"I'm not the best bird watcher in the world."

"You broke me into the business. That's good enough. How about it?"

Somehow — for once in his life, maybe — David had a feeling he had said just the right thing.

Chapter 8

*I*F the days came and went like tides, Vanessa thought, the summer itself had become like the sea: calm and lazy, drowning the world under its fragrant warmth.

The Bottoms swung and swirled with currents of colors: yellows of mullein and loosestrife; blues of chicory and vervain and Oswego tea; reds of wild roses, and purple-reds of milkweeds and thistles. And over and above these, the hovering, dancing colors of butterflies, damselflies and fat, pollen-heavy bumblebees. And each new morning the spilled-diamond colors of dewed spider webs in the grass.

There was the rich summer color of her own skin.

Charlotte marveled. "You never been so brown in your life, Baby."

Vanessa, pleased, stopped combing her hair. "You think so, Charlotte?" She looked into the mirror. It was true. She *was* tanned. And the way her hair was bleaching out in the sun made her skin even darker.

"Grandma wouldn't know you if she walked in today. Sometimes I don't myself, and that's a fact."

"How do you mean, Char?"

"The way you've done changed." She shook her head. "When I think of the way it was with you when school was out. Alone all the time, reading and reading and blowing your mind with it. And then that night you had that first bad dream. Baby, you was almost over the deep end there for a while. Remember?"

"Not very well." Vanessa began combing her hair again. "That's the funny thing. I really don't remember too much of it. It's all like a dream, sort of, something that really didn't happen. Anyway, it's over now."

"Thanks to David."

"And the birds and — everything."

"But mostly David."

"Yes."

"You probably ain't never had a friend before. I mean a boy, near your own age."

Vanessa shook her head. "I'm not too good at making friends. Except now. With David." She stopped combing. "You know something, Char? This may seem awful — but if, like, Gram wrote me a letter and said, 'You can either come down here with me, or you can stay with Charlotte until I come home' — if she gave me a choice like that, I don't think I'd go. I'd choose to stay here with you — and David — until she came back. Is that awful to say?"

"No."

"It seems kind of awful, but I can't help it. That's the way it is."

"Ain't nothing wrong about it I can see. You're happy and you want to keep on being happy. Gram'd be the first to understand that. Fact is, she'd probably be pleased you was growing up and making it on your own like this without her."

"You think so, Char?"

"I know so."

"Anyway, it won't be much longer. The letter I got yesterday, Gram said she was finally getting some order into the house there. That's a good sign. It means there won't be too much for her to do anymore and she'll be back soon."

"So there's nothing you have to do now 'cept relax and enjoy it, right?"

"Right."

"And that first day she walks in and gets a look at you . . ." Charlotte chuckled. "You know what you remind me of, Baby? Them coloring books where there's a picture of some little kid and it says 'Color me happy' — that's you right now. The color of happy."

But not just me, Vanessa thought. Everything was the color of happy.

There was nothing big or emotional about it. It was a quiet kind of happiness. So quiet she didn't even think about it most of the time. It was just there, that was all. Like a shield. Except that it wasn't exactly a shield either. It didn't keep you from getting hurt. Things could still break through and get to you. Things did. Like the baby mallard.

It happened that a leak at a refinery one morning drifted a swathe of oil across the river — not enough to require a log boom to contain it, but still enough to trap one small duckling unable to swim fast enough to escape it. The oil flowed around the duckling, gumming its baby down and small feathers. It dove under the water in an effort to escape, only to lose its direction and come up again in an even heavier portion of the slick. Then, its eyes clotted shut and its air passages sealed, the oil dragging away what little strength remained in its wings and webbed feet, it drifted to shore just below the dike.

Where Vanessa found it, a black, sodden ooze — scarcely in the form of a bird anymore, but still feebly stirring.

She and David had tried to remove the oil, first with cotton from David's medical stores, then with cotton and rubbing alcohol. And, miraculously, the duckling seemed to respond. It freed its small wings and spread them, it lifted its head, turning it about as though to catch some point of light through its oil-blinded eyes. It was the eyes that made Vanessa frantic, the thought of the bird alone in the darkness it did not understand.

"Can't you get them to open?" she cried almost angrily.

"I'm doing the best I can." And he was. She could see that. His hands on the bird were more gentle and sure than her own would have been. But the eyes weren't opening. "I can't use the alcohol near them," he said. "Look, mix me a glass of baking soda and water, and bring me some fresh cotton." He sponged gently at the eyes. Still they did not open. He dried the duckling carefully, then dusted it with dry soda. "Let's let it rest for a while," he said. "I'll bathe the eyes again later."

But later didn't matter because the duckling died. Its blind head slipped forward limply, then to one side and, like that, it was gone. They buried it in the field outside the tent. And with that, for the first time — very simply and quietly — death entered her life.

It entered again with cold, massive indifference.

One morning a dredge moved into shore, hoisted a large pipe to the top of the dike and began pumping. All day the sludge from the river bottom gouted into the pit. Near the mouth of the pipe it built up against the slanting wall of the dike. It was late in the afternoon when the pipe was raised and swung back aboard the dredge, and the summer stillness again washed over the pit. David looked across at the gray-black delta of muck where the pipe had been. The muck had buried one of the smaller marshes and

72

was already creeping into the lake. He swore in a low voice.

"It looks horrible," Vanessa said.

"It *is* horrible. Every time they do this, they kill off a little part of the pit. Okay, I know that's what they built it for, to pump mud in — but even so, a million things are living in it." He kicked at a loose rock, tumbling it down the face of the dike. "The marsh down there is gone now, all that border vegetation along the shore. The flowers, the fish, the insects, everything — it's a whole chain of killing, and once it starts, it keeps going on of itself."

And at that moment the chain reached Vanessa.

There were no swallows over the pit!

She was running along the top of the dike. Running toward something she did not want to see and did not dare to believe. She heard David calling after her but did not stop. She stopped only when she reached the place where the dredge pipe had rested.

She did not see the sludge, which had backed up the wall of the dike almost to her feet. She saw only the remembered holes now buried under the sludge, the holes filled with swallows and nestlings.

The holes sealed tight and forever under the mud.

It seemed to her that through the earth of the dike she could hear the swallows calling. Under the earth she could see, could feel the tiny bodies squirming and beating wings.

She did not feel her own hands and arms groping down through the heavy ooze; did not feel David dragging her out of it; did not feel him holding her, as she fought him, until her strength gave out. It was only later, back in the tent, when sense began coming back to her, that she began to feel.

And she did not think she would be able to bear it.

But in a day or two the horror of it wore off. What had

73

happened to the swallows even seemed, in a way, to take its place in an order of things. Just as the death of the baby mallard had taken its place.

She did not know what these places were, or what their meaning might be. Only that they were there, and that somehow there was a pattern in the way they fitted together.

And the strangest thing in the pattern was that these things, for all the pain and sadness they had brought her, were part of the deep, drifting happiness of the summer itself.

That was the way the summer went by, a slow drift of days into days — all much the same, yet each in its way somewhat different. Every morning Vanessa would come down to The Bottoms, and every afternoon toward dusk David would walk her back to the house. Sometimes after dark they would walk up Front Street for sundaes, or watch TV with Charlotte, or go to a movie. Sometimes they would merely sit on the front porch and talk, or not talk. That was all. Nothing much. Each day like the day before it, and like the day to come. Each night David, at some point, saying "Well, guess I'd better be going," but making no move to go.

He didn't have to, of course. He knew that. Charlotte had said "You can stay here, we got plenty of room." And Vanessa kept coaxing him to stay. And in a way he wanted to. But in a stronger way he wanted to be back in the tent, quiet among the quiet sounds of the night and the river.

Once Vanessa asked him, "Aren't you afraid?"

"Of what?" he replied, genuinely surprised.

"Of going down there. In the dark. Alone."

"There's nothing to be afraid of." Which had startled him. Not the fact that he had said it, but that it was true.

He *wasn't* afraid. Things had changed from the way they had been in the beginning.

All the old fears were gone. He was no longer troubled by the darkness, the sounds of the darkness, the ominous presence of the pit; he no longer minded being alone under the night. Everything was different now.

Not that the reason wasn't simple enough: by facing these things he had learned to live with them; it had happened before.

Except that that was only part of the reason.

The other part — although he didn't like to admit it because it was maybe the more important part — was Vanessa. Just the fact that she was around. But why this should make such a difference he did not know.

Maybe it was because they were friends, because for once he had found someone who cared about the things he cared about, and who shared with him what happened each day no matter what happened. Maybe a thing as simple as this had the power to put all the things his imagination frightened him with in their proper and sensible place. Although that wasn't entirely true either. He was still himself, afraid of many things and somehow compelled to magnify them beyond what they were. No use kidding himself about that. But now it was as though they were in some way outside him, not inside where they caused all the trouble. They were far out, beyond the night even. They were at bay.

And it was Vanessa who seemed to be keeping them there.

Chapter 9

FROM the standpoint of weather, most of the days were good. That is, they were clear and sunny, with the prevailing wind from the west and northwest.

There were bad days, though, when the wind slipped around to the southwest, and the smoke from the furnaces and fumes from the refineries rolled like a river over The Bottoms. On those days, when their eyes burned and the acrid air seemed to back up in their lungs, the project became an actual hardship.

"I don't see why we have to stay," Vanessa complained. "There's no point to it."

"That's just the point. That's what the whole project is all about — to see how this sort of thing affects The Bottoms."

"But it's stupid to stay when nothing is happening."

"How will we know what's happening unless we're here? You can go if you want to, Vanessa, and then come back when the wind shifts around."

"No, I'll stay."

For the most part, on those days, they remained in the tent, protected to some extent from the smoke and fumes. It was even fun in a way, Vanessa discovered, because it was a little like playing house. She allowed herself to pretend at times that she and David were grown up and married, and that he was a scientist engaged in an important study at some remote and lonely outpost. The tent was their home and it was her job to take care of both him and the home.

She did not tell David about it because it was her own private game. Besides, she thought, it would only embarrass him.

Even though it was still August, there were days when fall seemed near.

It had nothing to do with the temperature, for it was still summer-hot; nothing to do with changing colors, for the woods and fields were still green. It was merely a feeling sometimes that the heavy massed foliage of the trees was too heavy, that the woods themselves were tired. The shy, gentle yellows of early summer wildflowers were now feverish, bright yellows. All along the edges of the woods, sunflowers and goldenrod seemed to be burning.

It was still summer, but it was ending too. And there was a sadness about it that wasn't there before. Vanessa knew that part of the sadness was because of David. He was restless and moody, wandering alone about the pit the greater part of each day.

"It's the sandpipers," he finally explained. "They're late, and there's no good reason for it. Last year at this time there'd be fifty to a couple hundred feeding down there around the lakes."

"Maybe this is what our study is proving — that they're not coming here anymore."

"They were here in the spring. The pollution factor was worse then. No, they're late in migration and I can't figure out why."

"Supposing they're on schedule, only they're not coming here. I mean they might be somewhere else along the river."

"But we don't know that. All we know is what we see right here."

"Couldn't we find out?"

"I don't know how."

"You said once there was an Audubon Society in town. Maybe if you called them they'd know."

But it was worse after he knew.

"They're here all right," he said gloomily. "About twenty miles upstream along the rapids, and all around the bay. Good reports from all over."

"It has to be pollution then, doesn't it?"

"What else?"

"Maybe they'll still come, though. It's early in the season."

"Not anymore. No way." There was something in his face, something deeper than disappointment. Vanessa wanted to understand it.

"Does it matter so much?" she asked hesitantly.

"I was hoping they'd come, that's all."

"But why them any more than the others?"

He did not answer at once. "I suppose," he said at last, "because they're my favorite birds." He looked out over the pit. "That's how I got started birdwatching. Through sandpipers. Most people start out with the birds they see in their back yards, the jays and robins and juncos. Me, I started with sandpipers. They were my backyard birds on account of our place on the Cape. Maybe that's why I've always watched for sandpipers no matter where we lived. They always brought back the Cape, they were like home. So I suppose, now, not coming back . . ." He shrugged and did not finish.

And then early one evening, after Vanessa had gone, it happened.

A solitary pectoral sandpiper circled the pit and touched down on a sandbar in the smaller lake. And that night David heard them, the *whee-whee-whee-whee's* of the yellowlegs and the thrilling *threeps* of the least sandpipers.

"They were here," he told Vanessa excitedly the next morning. "They're gone now, but they did come last night."

"Maybe tonight they'll come again."

"Maybe, maybe."

"Can I stay and watch with you?"

"You mean in the tent?"

"Yes."

"Charlotte wouldn't let you."

"Yes she would."

"You know damn well she wouldn't."

"Would you like me to?"

"Sure I'd like you to, but . . ."

"Then I'll ask her."

"It won't do any good."

"Let's ask her together."

"No use, Vannie, save your breath."

Vanessa pleaded. Charlotte said no.

David ventured the opinion that it would be nice if Vanessa could see what it was like down there at night.

Charlotte said no.

Vanessa went on pleading. David began to look pained. "I said no and I mean no," Charlotte snapped. "Neither of you know what you're asking."

And then, even as she said it, the startling thought struck her: *neither of them did know.*

She was the one who was wrong here. She was measuring Vanessa against herself at Vanessa's age — and measuring David against her son, Josh. And you couldn't measure like that because the yardstick wasn't the same. She had grown up fast, and Josh even faster. At age eleven, back in Alabama, if she had dared to ask Mama to spend a night in a tent with a boy, Mama would have belted her — and with good reason. Mama knew her girl. And if Josh had come around with the same request, there'd have been an even bigger belting because Josh was a wild one. But these two? She grinned all at once, unable to hide it. These two were still dumb, or innocent, or both. They were still interested in *things*, things like their crazy birds. They hadn't begun thinking about each other. At least not in that way.

It was the very fact that they *didn't* know what they were asking that made everything all right.

She gathered a handful of Vanessa's sun-bleached hair and gave it a rough tug. "Oh, go along if you want to," she said. "It's okay."

"We sure picked a lousy night," David said.

It was hot and sultry, an oven of a night. No breeze stirred. The lights of the city bounced back from the heat haze overhead, making the darkness almost daylight. The surface of the river, still as glass, burned under the flames of the blast furnaces.

"It doesn't matter," Vanessa said.

"It does, though. No birds will come tonight."

"Even if they don't, it's fun. For me anyway."

"But I wanted you to be here on a good night. When it's really beautiful down here."

"Don't worry about it, David. I'm not."

"It may storm. That could change things." He cleared off

the cot and unrolled a sleeping bag on the tent floor. "You take the cot," he said. "I'll take the bag."

"I don't mind sleeping in the bag."

"I'll take the bag." He grinned at her, a little uncertainly. "We might as well sack in. There's nothing else to do." He blew out the candle. In the pale light in the tent she saw him looking at her. She could feel something anxious about him.

"What's the matter?" she asked.

"Nothing." But he stood there, troubled by something. "Look," he said finally, "if you want to undress or something, I'll go out. But you don't really have to. I mean, I just sleep in my clothes. You can too if you want."

"I'm not *going* to undress."

"Okay." She sensed relief in his voice. "No problem then. Let's turn in."

She might have dozed off, or she might have just lain there, snug and contented, thinking about nothing in particular. But when awareness came again, it was to the sound of approaching thunder and the churning of wind through the trees. The tent exploded in lightning. She sat up, frightened.

"David?"

She felt a hand reaching up from the floor. She clutched the hand.

"Don't be afraid," he said sleepily. "The tent's waterproof. We'll be all right."

She lay back, reassured, and listened to the storm coming. It was coming fast; the rain in the distance was like a heavy wet whisper filling the night. The whisper grew louder, swelling as it came down the river toward them. It burst over the tent like the pouring of tons of gravel. Vanessa lay rigid, waiting for the tent to collapse. But it held. After a while the gravel lessened; the stones of rain-drops seemed to grow smaller and lighter; then they turned to fine falling sand. At last they fell in a soft and steady, dreaming hush.

Somewhere, deep under the hush, someone was shaking her.

She thought it was Charlotte and crawled deeper into her small cave of sleep. The shaking continued, she heard her name being called. Gradually she remembered where she was and who was calling.

"Get up!" David's whisper was fierce, excited. "They're here."

She opened her eyes. And at the same time became aware of sounds. Sounds, at first, of trickling waters, of an immense wetness as though the whole earth was drip-ping. Then slowly, above these sounds, the thin clittering sounds of birds.

"Come on, get your shoes on. Let's go." David was standing impatiently by the cot, a folded tarpaulin under his arm. She thrust into her sneakers and quickly tied them. David propelled her out of the tent. Into a night that almost took her breath away.

Gone was the heat, the haze, the humidity. The sky was a blue-black ocean swirling with brilliant currents of stars. The river was rolling under the wind, laden with broken jewels of lights along its shoreline. And everywhere, though invisible, were the sandpipers.

She followed David to the top of the dike and helped him spread the tarpaulin. Then they watched. The lakes in the pit were still; they held the stars like motionless schools of fish. The sandpipers could not be seen, but their pres-ence was a living, pulsating force filling the pit. Their thin piping cries rose and fell in a ceaseless, unearthly music.

Vanessa stretched out on the tarpaulin and stared up into the night.

It was cool now, and the air smelled of the rain that had passed. The sky, like a dirty window, had been washed by the rain and there were stars in it she had never seen before: millions upon millions of them tumbled across the night. And they too seemed wet and washed and dripping with light. As her eyes adjusted to it, and her mind began to find its way in it, she could dimly make out sudden swift passages of birds.

David, lying beside her, said, "The yellowlegs — that's the *weet-weet-weet* cry — they've been coming from Hudson's Bay and beyond, and they'll be going on down, some of them, below the equator as far as Chile. And traveling at night. Think of it."

She thought of it. She lifted her mind high, and higher and higher into the night, shrinking herself into the form of a bird. She let herself coast, wings outstretched, between the great blocks and triangles of blue constellations, feeling the rain-sweet air flowing past and under her. Overhead and all around were the great coastlines of stars, and down below, the jeweled lights of the city and the broken-jeweled lights of the long, dark river.

Sometime later — she lost track of time — they folded up the tarpaulin and returned to the tent.

Vanessa did not sleep. She merely waited for daybreak to come.

When it did come — before the sun was fully up and the light was still bluish and cool — she slipped out of the tent while David was still asleep, waded through the wet field grass and climbed to the top of the dike.

The sandpipers were still there, hundreds of them, thronging, feeding, taking off and landing again. There was

83

no sound in the world but their soft weetling cries. The city was still. The Bottoms were still. The river was still as the cloudless sky. In a stillness within her that was even deeper than these, she felt herself moving down toward the birds and then among them, and holding out her arms and gathering them to her. It was as though, having been with them in the night, she was one with them. She belonged now to their world and their morning.

She sat on the dike in the morning stillness, letting her love go out to them. And out and out. There was no end to it. It seemed to her she had reached some high point of happiness, which she did not know how to handle. That all of the summer — which had been more wonderful than anything she had ever known before — had been moving toward just this point. And now it was here. And she was here. The sun was rising, the whole world was coming slowly alight. It was as though it was happening for the first time in creation, and it was happening only for her.

She sat in the rising sun, letting herself flow out and belong to everything in the world.

Chapter 10

*T*HEN the world ended.

It ended because one day a man and his son went down into the pit to fish.

David and Vanessa, perched on top of the dike, watched them coming through the field, each carrying a long cane pole and a tackle box.

"Who are these characters?" David growled.

"I don't know. They're just going fishing, I suppose."

"I've never seen them before."

"So?"

David glowered at her, then at the two figures who were climbing the slope of the dike.

"After all," Vanessa said, "we don't own the place, do we?"

"No, but . . ."

David was unreasonable at times. He seemed to think no one had a right to be in The Bottoms except themselves. He raised his glasses and began scanning the pit, pretending to watch something so that he would not have to make conversation.

"Don't act like this!" she hissed.

The pair came toward them, a large jolly-faced man and a white-haired boy with two sunburn smudges on his cheeks.

"Hi, kids," the man said.

David did not look up. Vanessa knew he would not speak.

"Hi," she said.

"How's the fishing down there?"

"I don't know. We don't fish. David, do you know?"

David took his time about lowering the glasses. He did not bother to look up. "There's fish, I guess. Crappies, blue gills."

"The kids in the neighborhood say it's pretty good."

David shrugged.

"We'll try it anyway and see," the man said.

David started to raise the glasses again, then stopped. "I'd be careful if I were you. There's a lot of soft ground down there, especially after a rain."

"It looks dry enough to me."

"The crust is dry but it's soft underneath."

The man laughed and clapped the boy's shoulder. "So we get a little mud on our feet."

"It's deep mud and dangerous."

"We'll watch it. Thanks for the warning."

They watched the pair make their way down the dike into the pit.

"Wise guy," David grunted. "Knows everything."

"He seemed kind of nice."

"Jerk."

"Why do you have to be so mean sometimes?"

"Because I'm mean." He stood up abruptly. "Let's go."

"Maybe we'd better wait a little."

"Why?"

"To see if, you know, if they're all right."

"They'll be all right. That's a big-time explorer down there. He knows all the trails."

"I think we should wait."

"I said come on! I want to see if any peeps are feeding along the river."

They climbed down the dike into the field. It was like wading out into an ocean of color. Asters and goldenrod were chest-high now. Ragweed and tick trefoil brushed their chins. Thistles and burdock were over their heads. They had to search before they found the path to the river. Grasshoppers shuttled before them, the fields throbbed with crickets. Over the sound of the crickets, Vanessa thought she heard another sound.

"David?"

He halted.

"Did you hear that?"

"Hear what?"

"Like someone calling."

"I didn't hear anything."

"There it is again!"

"I didn't hear anything," he said gruffly.

"I'm going to have a look."

He caught her arm. "Nobody was calling, Vannie. What's your trouble?"

"They were. I heard them!"

"You didn't hear anything. There was nothing to hear."

She jerked her arm free. "At least look, will you? It won't hurt you to do that."

He made a disgusted face, kicked through the field and climbed to the top of the dike. When he returned, he barely glanced at her. "Nothing," he said curtly. "Let's get going."

They made their way to the river and poked along the shore. Presently David spotted a flock of least sandpipers feeding there. They watched them for a while. "Let me use the glasses," Vanessa said. She focused on the sandpipers. "I'm there too, David. Me and another dunlin. Did you see us?" She raised the glasses and looked along the shoreline beyond the birds, then out across the river. Then, turning, looked back at the dike.

"David, look!" she cried. "Up there!"

The man and the boy were walking along the top of the dike. They were walking strangely, with heavy, dragging steps. They had neither their poles nor their tackle boxes.

Vanessa adjusted the center-focus of the glasses. She caught her breath sharply. "They're all mud! The man up to his waist. The little boy's all covered with it. They must have broken through. Here, take a look." She turned and held out the glasses.

David had not moved from the boulder where he was sitting. He was staring at her. "Here," she repeated. He did not reach out to take the glasses. "You were right. You warned them. They should have listened to you."

He looked at her, his eyes growing wider and wider.

She was suddenly afraid. "Don't you want to look?"

And then a terrible thing happened. David began to cry.

After that, everything began coming apart.

The way, each year, the ice on the river began coming apart. First, the big, long cracks; then the cracks splintering out into other cracks; then all of them widening until the ice began breaking into drifting floes.

This was the way the days were now: as though she was on one floe and David on another and they were drifting further apart. So far apart that she could no longer call to him anymore and make him hear her.

And there was no reason for any of it.

But reason or no, something had happened. David was definitely avoiding her. He spent most of each day wandering aimlessly about the pit. Sometimes he would lie for

88

hours in the tent, eyes open and staring, but staring at nothing. And there seemed nothing she could do except watch and wonder, sick at heart, what it might be that was wrong.

Something had to be done.

She set herself coldly to think it out.

When did it begin? It had to be that day with the man and his son. There had been nothing before; she was certain of this. So it had to be that day.

But what happened that day?

And again she was up against the same answer. Nothing. True, the man and the boy had broken through the mud. But David had warned them. And they had gotten out. So nothing had really happened.

Except that David had started crying. And everything good and real between them had begun breaking up. There was no reason for it. None. But it was still happening. It was getting worse, and she did not know what it was or how to stop it.

At last there was only one way left to her, the one she dreaded to take.

She went into the tent. David was lying on the cot, hands folded on his chest, staring up at the tent roof. She looked down at him.

"What is it David?"

He did not answer.

"David?"

No answer.

"We're friends. You can tell me."

He closed his eyes. "Go away, Vanessa. Leave me alone."

"Is it what happened that day? With the man and the little boy?"

"I said leave me alone."

"It wasn't your fault what happened. You warned them."
She waited for him to say something. "You did what you
could," she said. "It wasn't your fault they didn't listen.
And besides, they got out all right; nothing happened.
There's nothing you have to blame yourself for."

He looked at her. She had never seen eyes so steady in
torment. He covered his face with both hands.

"All right," he said, "you want to know, I'll tell you." His
voice was flat, without any feeling. "I heard the cry that
day. I said I didn't, but I did. When you said I should go up
and look —" He stopped. His mouth turned downward
hard, against his teeth as though he was about to be sick.
"When I looked — they were both in the mud. Fighting it. I
came back down. I pretended I hadn't seen it. I'm afraid
of the pit, the mud. You know that. I've never made a secret
of it." He stopped again and swallowed. "I knew I should
have gone to help them — but I was afraid, so I didn't do
it. I let them go. They got out all right, but as far as I'm
concerned, they really didn't. They died down there. I saw
it happening and I let them die. I didn't know then that
they'd get out, I didn't think they would. But I walked
away from them anyway. And there's no way to make it
right any more."

He let his hands fall and turned his face from her. "Now
you know," he said. "Now leave me alone."

She stared down at him. She was not thinking about
what he told her. Something very calm in her said not to
think. Later, perhaps, but not now. It was like turning out
a light; she had flicked a switch and thinking had stopped.
But she did look at him. He seemed very small and slight.
Too slight for the burden of guilt crushing down on him.

"David," she whispered, "I'm going now."

He nodded silently.

She bent and kissed his forehead. "I'll be back though. I'm staying here tonight."

Charlotte listened.

She listened quietly without once interrupting. Even when the whole story was out and nothing more left to tell, she didn't say anything for a long while. At last she sighed.

"What can I say, Baby? Except I know what you're feeling. When you was in trouble — not that it was near as bad as this — it was the same thing with you and me."

Vanessa shook her head. "It was different with us, Char. I wanted help. I came to you. David doesn't want help. He keeps pulling away from me."

"What does his daddy say 'bout this?"

"He doesn't know. He's on one of those long trips of his. In Texas or someplace."

"David must know how to reach him."

"He doesn't want to. I asked him for his father's phone number, but he won't give it to me. Char, what am I going to do?"

Charlotte looked at her; for a very long while, it seemed. At last she said, very gently. "What you going to do? You going to do the hardest thing in the world, girl. Nothing. Except let go. That's what I did with you after a while. I kept my eye on you, but let you go your own way. And you got to do the same. He's a real troubled boy. He's done something he can't forgive himself for. You can't forgive him and nobody else can. He's going to have to work out some way of doing it himself, and you got to let him do it. Don't pester him, don't tag around after him. Just look after him and let him find his own way out."

So she did.

She no longer followed him when he wandered about in the pit, or sat on the river bank monotonously pitching stones in the water, or disappeared for hours at a time in the woods. But she knew where he was. Always, at any given moment. She kept the tent clean, maintained the food supply, made sure that he ate. She took charge of the bird count and kept the records up to date. Once, when a sudden storm broke, she made her way through the downpour into the woods where she found him seated on a log, head buried in his arms.

"Come, David," she said gently and took him by the hand. He allowed himself to be led back to the tent. While she was drying him off with a bath towel, he looked about him, almost in surprise, and remarked "It's raining, isn't it?"

She knew then that very soon, if nothing changed, he would need a kind of help she could no longer give him.

And she knew that nothing now would change.

Chapter 11

*B*UT it did change.

And the change was as swift and brutal as the blow of a fist.

The afternoon was hot and hazy, almost too bright. The two lakes in the pit, cleansed by recent rains, were a blinding glare, their shorelines and the mud crust itself a sheen of dust. David and Vanessa were sitting together on the dike, silent, for they had reached the point where they had nothing to talk about anymore. They might have been two strangers.

They watched a gull circling the larger lake. A Bonaparte gull with a small black smudge behind each eye. It was a swift, graceful bird, its pattern of flight closer to that of a swallow than to that of the heavier, slow-beating herring gulls. It flew out over the lake, then back toward the shoreline. It suddenly checked as it glimpsed a minnow, and plunged toward the surface of the water. Which turned out not to be surface, but instead a too-glaring strip of gravel at the lake's edge.

The gull crashed, rolled over, tried to rise, and tumbled across the gravel trailing a broken wing. The wing was not merely broken, it was partially separated from the body. Then the tip of the wing caught on something and pulled further apart.

The gull lay motionless in its pain.

What had happened seemed to have been going on for hours. It had not taken more than fifteen seconds.

Vanessa whispered shakily, "David, what should we . . .?"

But David was standing, his eyes fixed on the gravel bar.

"We can't let it stay out there," he said in a low voice. "I'll have to try and get it."

"You can't! The ground in between is too wet."

He did not take his eyes from the gull. "I think I can make it if it stays on the bar."

"David, no!"

"There's a plank down there. I'll carry it in case." His face was very pale. "What I want you to do is this. Go to the tent. Get the little bottle of chloroform in the medicine chest. We'll have to put the bird away afterward, it's too badly hurt. Get the chloroform. Then keep your eye on me. If you see I'm in trouble, go for help. Your best bet is the fire station. Get them as fast as you can."

She caught at him. "No! Don't, please!"

But he was already sliding down the bank to the muddy shore.

The plank was nearly five feet long and a foot across. Large enough. He had done it once before on a survival exercise, crossing a spread of muddy tidal flat. He knew what to do. That time he hadn't been afraid; it had even been fun in a way. But he hadn't been alone then. And it was a different kind of mud. No use thinking about that now. If he were lucky . . .

He scanned the stretch of mud between himself and the gravel bar. It looked dry, it could be dryer than he thought. It was already cracked in good solid fissures.

He stepped onto it. It held his weight. He could feel its

94

deep, unsteady tremble, but it was reasonably solid. He took a deep breath and started toward the bar, plotting his way carefully. Suddenly his right foot sank, not far, but enough. He pulled it out, drew back in fear.

No use. Impossible. He'd have to turn back.

But that was the thing, wasn't it? He had always turned back. From everything. He was a coward, and this was why he was a coward: nothing was more important than himself.

He stood, sweating in fear, unable to move forward or back. The gull moved slightly on the bar; he could see the bright blood on the stones beneath it. Something in the concentrated pain of the white body seemed all at once more compelling than himself.

He stepped forward. Went down. He slogged forward, sinking with each step. Each step harder to withdraw. The smell of the broken mud was raw and damp; it smelled like sewer gas. The fear was steady now, thick, clotting his skin like mud. He plodded toward the bar. The bird, frightened, began stirring. "Steady," he murmured to it in a choked voice. "Don't be afraid, I'm not going to hurt you." He moved toward it. But the gull began beating away from him, dragging itself off the bar and out onto a part of the mudfield beyond that was still damp.

He stopped, his heart pounding so that it seemed he must faint.

No use. I can't go on.

He went on.

Taking a step, sinking, pulling his other leg from the mud with a squelching sound and taking another step. And sinking again. The mud rose slowly up his legs. There was no solidity of any kind any more. He was wallowing through a sea of black dough.

Suddenly he sank down over his knees, caught his breath with a cry. Stopped. Felt himself slowly sinking.

95

Collapsed bent over, face downward, onto the plank. He waited for a few moments. Then slowly, carefully, he rocked his body to one side in the mud, pushed the plank ahead of him and drew himself onto it. He lay there, his breath sobbing through his lungs. Then he rocked off, slid the plank ahead, and pulled himself onto it again.

He struggled on toward the gull that way, on belly and hands and knees, pushing the plank and crawling onto it. Each time having to rest a little longer, gasping for breath. The mud clung to his skin and clothing, began packing into a heavy sheath of clay armor. It weighed him further, but there was no way of scraping it off. He dragged it along with him, blindly now, a worm crawling through mud. But near the goal. He must be close now. He raised his head and peered about.

He saw the gull, still far out.

Too far beyond him.

He rested his face in the slime on the board, exhausted, the pit swaying and sucking under him.

Something in him quietly gave up.

The firemen raced after her, four of them, carrying rope, a ladder, a stretcher. "Hurry," she wailed, "please hurry." But when she reached the top of the dike she saw nothing. Nothing in the pit, nothing in the mud.

And then, beyond the gravel bar, she saw a small mound that was not mud.

"There!" She pointed. "Out there! See him!"

The firemen plunged down the dike ahead of her. She would have followed, but her legs gave out suddenly. She fell on the bank, burying her face in the weeds. She was crying, but without tears. Only with sounds so painful they seemed like roots being torn from her chest. When at last she dared to look up, she saw that the men had reached the bar and one of them, carrying the rope, was working his way through the mud beyond on the ladder. She saw the rope coil out, saw a muddy arm reach out for its tangles, grasp it. Saw the rope begin to tighten.

He was safe on the shore of the lake when she reached them. A thing of mud. Only his eyes were alive in the mud. A dead muddy gull lay on the shore beside him; the firemen must have brought it in too. One of the firemen rolled him onto his stomach, turned his head to one side and dug clots of mud from his mouth. Sounds came with the mud. She broke through the men and flung herself beside him.

"David — David!"

The sounds kept coming. She bent her head to his face. "Chloroform." She barely made out the word. "Bird. Chloroform."

She touched his hair. "Yes," she said.

One of the firemen lifted her. "The best thing you can do now is go home," he said gently. "We'll get him to the hospital. Metropolitan. You can come there later."

She looked at the fireman wordlessly, afraid to ask.

"He'll be all right. We'll notify his father. You just go now — and don't worry."

They lifted David onto the stretcher, then hoisted it between them.

"Run along now," the fireman urged her. "Everything's all right."

When she turned the corner she saw Charlotte there on the porch, and then she was running toward her and the next moment her arms were about her and she was sobbing the whole thing out.

Charlotte held her, rocking her gently. At first Charlotte tried to say something, but then she merely held her, listening, stroking her hair.

97

And then — only then — did Vanessa become aware of a man standing on the porch looking at her. A white man in a grimy T-shirt and faded jeans. The man looked uncomfortable. He cleared his throat. Vanessa looked at Charlotte.

Charlotte said very quietly, "Vannie, this is your Uncle Mart. He's come to take you back with him."

Fear seemed to paralyze her. She heard the word "Back?" escape from her lips.

Uncle Mart came closer. "Grandma sent me down to get you, Vanessa. We've got to get rolling."

"I can't! Not now. With David."

Charlotte looked at Uncle Mart. She turned so that she blocked Uncle Mart out. "You have to, Vannie," she said softly. "You have to. There's no other way."

"I won't! No!"

"I've packed everything, Baby. It's loaded in the car. All you do is git in and go now. Right away, no thinking about it. It's the best way."

"No!" She tried to break away, but Charlotte was holding her. "He's in the hospital. I've got to go to the hospital."

"I'll go to the hospital for you. I'll tell David what happened and why you couldn't come. He'll understand. And I'll write to you. I'll let you know how things are."

Vanessa screamed then. In hopelessness. In rage. Against the emptiness that was filling her as though something in her had been killed. She tore free of Charlotte and began running. Arms caught her, whirled her hard against a too-powerful body, into a tired smell of sweat and tobacco. She fought the body and the smell until she no longer could.

She was hysterical when at last she was carried to the waiting car.

Chapter 12

FOR a little while things simply happened.

There was Gram to begin with — and when they turned into the yard and Gram came running out to the car, Vanessa's heart gave a wonderfully wild leap and, for the first time, she forgot about David. Then there was the houseful of cousins to meet. And Aunt Rachel who was both big as a house and as radiant as a well-lived-in house. Even Uncle Mart turned out to be not so grim after all, but in fact very quiet and sweet. For a little while in the beginning, the world was so new and the days so full that she scarcely thought about David at all. When she did, he seemed almost too far away and long ago to remember clearly. But then the world became itself again and the newness wore off.

And she remembered.

She saw — it was as though she had not noticed before — that West Virginia was all hills. They surrounded the house and the village. It was not like Ohio, where the sky came down to the land, where — when you looked out toward the bay — there was only a thin line between sky and water, and everywhere was blue and heavenly space. Here, the hills blocked out most of the sky; it was like living inside a cup. And there was no river here. There was a little creek that came down from the hills in spring, but its bed was dry now and full of weeds and rubbish. There were birds, but not the white gulls. Nor the brown, pointed-winged sandpipers that seemed to carry the sea and the stars with them in their lovely flighting. There was no space to move in, or breathe in; no water for the heart to love.

And beyond all else, no David.

And no promised letter.

Only the day-after-day waiting for Uncle Mart to come home from the post office. With nothing. Nothing at all.

And then one day it did come. Addressed only to her. She carried it out behind the garage where, for a few minutes anyway, she knew she would be alone. With shaking fingers she opened the envelope.

Dear Vannie —

I am sorry I have not wrote before but have been so busy with things.

Anyway David he is O.K. He was sick for a while and did not start school when he should of, but he has started now. He misses you lots, ha-ha. He will be glad when you get back. I gave him your address and he says he will write you. He says tell you the birds are gone now, most of them. Except the white ones, the sea gulls.

Say hello to Grandma for me. I hope you come back soon. Keep up the old chin, Baby.

> *Love*
> *Charlotte*

And suddenly everything was right again. Everything was in place. When she looked up, even the hills were lower and the sky was almost as high and wide as it was at home. She knew, no matter how long things lasted, she could wait them out.

When school started it was a breeze; she was so far ahead of her class that there was no need even to study. And then in October the baby came and Aunt Rachel made out all right. Soon she was home from the hospital, and about the same time Uncle Mart got a job driving a truck on a run between Charleston and Wheeling.

And then one day, the dreamed-of day she had never thought would come, Gram began packing again.

It was on a Saturday afternoon, early in November, that the taxi pulled up in front of the double-sided house again and they were home at last. It was a gray day, with a powder of snow sifting lazily down, but she saw neither the snow nor the grayness through the blinding white sun that was filling her. Then Charlotte was hurrying down the walk to them. There were cries, embracings, bags being gathered up. Vanessa hesitated, but only for a moment.

"I'll be back, Gram. In just a little while."

"Where are you going, Vannie?"

"I won't be long."

"But where are you going?"

"Just down to our place. I want to surprise David."

"Darling, at least change your clothes."

"I'll be careful, Gram, don't worry. 'Bye."

And she was on her way.

Running. Walking when she needed to catch her breath. Then running again.

Trying to imagine how it would be.

David would be down in the pit, and she would climb to the top of the dike and call, "David!" And he would turn around and see her, not able to believe it. Or he might be out along the river, and she would make her way through the fields and come up quietly behind him. Or he would be in the tent doing something, and he wouldn't see her at first, and she would stand there in the tent opening until he happened to look up. Or she would . . .

She would . . .

By the time she started down the path into The Bottoms she had given up the idea of playing games. There was no way of containing any longer the excitement inside her. When she glimpsed the faded green wall of the tent through the trees, she could only cry, "David, David." And as she ran toward it, "David, I'm here!" She broke through the tangle of brush about it.

And stopped abruptly.

A gigantic hand seemed to shove her breath back into her throat.

It couldn't be.

The tent hung loose, collapsed from the sagging ridge rope that held it. The canvas was torn, moldy. There was nothing inside but empty, overturned crates and boxes.

But it could not be.

She ran through the field and climbed to the top of the dike. She did not feel the wind. Her coat was open and her hair blowing about her face, but she did not feel the wind. "David!" she called. But he was not on the dike, not in the pit. She slid down the dike and fought her way through the high thistles and burdock to the river, calling, "David, David!" But there was no one anywhere.

She wanted to keep running, but could not. The weight crushing down on her was greater than her strength. Merely to walk was an effort. She stumbled back through The Bottoms.

The landlady at David's house opened the door. "Yes?"

"David — Is he here?"

The landlady looked at her strangely. "He don't live here no more. They moved."

"Do you know where — they moved?"

"I don't know. The father, he said something about In-iana. Or Illinois. I forget which. Anyway, they ain't here anymore."

The door closed. She stood there looking at it. She went on looking at it for a long while.

Then she turned and started home.

When she arrived home, Gram and Charlotte were sitting on the sofa. She looked at them mutely. There was nothing to say. The room was very still. Charlotte rose and came toward her. She stretched a hand and laid it against her cheek.

"You know?" Charlotte asked gently.

Vanessa nodded.

"I was going to tell you but you got away too fast."

"It doesn't matter," she lied.

"It was a week ago, maybe a little longer. David, he come over to tell me. That job his father had at the refinery, it was over. They went back home. Somewhere in the east."

"Wellfleet."

"That's it, Wellfleet. He said he'd write."

Vanessa nodded.

He would not write. She would not see him again. She knew this with a deep, weary certainty. This was the way it would be. She forced a smile. She had a feeling she should say something to go along with the smile, but nothing seemed worth saying. "I'm tired," was all she said. "I think I'll go upstairs and rest for a while."

In her room she stretched out on her bed and stared up at the ceiling. I can cry now, she thought. I don't have to hold up anymore.

But the tears would not come. She could not make them. And even if she could, it wouldn't matter, it wouldn't help any. The thing would still be there. The thing deep under all the tears she could ever cry.

That never . . .

Never ever would she see David again.

She turned her head on the pillow and looked through the window. It was gray outside, a thick, muddy gray. She could see it now. She could see the snow falling through the bare upper boughs of the trees. It is winter, she thought numbly; winter is beginning.

But by noon on Sunday, winter had warmed and melted away.

It remained only within herself.

She enrolled in junior high school the next day. Although she was six weeks behind in her courses, it was not a new experience for her. She had been even further behind when she had entered some schools in the past. In a couple or three weeks she would make up the work and be even with the rest of her class.

But in a couple of weeks she had made up nothing.

By December she was falling steadily behind.

When Mr. Melcher, her advisor, called her in for a conference, he glanced down at an open file on his desk.

"I've been going over your grades, Vanessa," he said. "It appears you were an excellent student all through elementary school. Particularly in Math and English — which is a rather unusual combination to be good in." He looked up and smiled. She could see that he was not an unkind person. "But I'm afraid that's not the case now, is it?"

"No."

"What's the trouble?"

"I don't know."

"Ordinarily I'd put it down to the fact that you started late. Under the best circumstances that's a rough hurdle to get over. But then this has happened to you before and you never seemed to have problems with it. Is it just junior high, perhaps — and the fact that you *are* somewhat younger than the rest of the students?"

She shook her head.

"Do you have any idea what the trouble might be?"

She stared at the file on Mr. Melcher's desk. Maybe it was because she was tired, she thought. She couldn't think well when she was tired. And thinking itself was tiresome. It was the snow too, maybe. Ever since she had watched the snow falling outside the window that day, it was as though it had gone on falling inside her. Everything — feeling, thinking — seemed buried under a gray, heavy snow. But she did not know how to explain this to Mr. Melcher, so she could only shrug.

"I guess I'll just have to try harder," she said, and let it go at that.

She did try — it was in her nature to try — but somehow it didn't work. Her mind didn't seem to hold things. And she really didn't care. It was as though something was missing in her, or numbed by the cold. Or had stopped. The summer itself was like something that had never happened. When she tried to remember it, to find her way back to it again, it kept slipping away from her. Even David.

Most of all, David. Sometimes she could not find him at all.

They had always talked of taking pictures: of the camp, of the pit, of each other; but they never had. They had been too busy with other things. So there were no pictures to help her in those awful times when she could not seem to remember what David looked like. There was no way back. Sometimes, walking home from school along Front Street, she would see a few winter gulls coasting

105

over the river, but they had no special meaning for her. Once, she stopped along the edge of The Bottoms and looked through the bare trees toward the dike. She did not know what she expected to feel, but she felt nothing. David, she thought, David, David.

But David was gone.

One day there was a conference with Mr. Melcher and Gram. "It's not entirely Vanessa's fault," Mr. Melcher explained kindly. "She started late. She *is* a good bit younger than the rest of her class. And the transition from elementary to junior high is often difficult for the best of students. So all these things are naturally against her. I'd say, though, that if her work doesn't start picking up, we should begin thinking in terms of having her repeat this year."

The work didn't pick up. She couldn't make it.

She merely rose each morning, went to school, returned home, switched on television and sometime later went to bed. She did not study, she did not read. She surrendered, uncaring, to time and allowed it to pass.

In a way it was all like one long day and one long night. January got mixed up in it. Then February. Then March. They were all the same. The snow kept falling inside her. There was no end to it.

One afternoon in April when she returned home, Gram met her at the door. "There's someone here to see you, Vanessa," she said gravely.

"Oh?" she replied without interest. She walked past Gram into the parlor. A man, a stranger, rose from the chair and smiled at her. He studied her for what seemed a long time.

"So you're Vanessa," he finally said.

"Yes."

"We should have met before, but somehow we never

did." He came across the room and took her hand. "I'm Don Pinkham," he said, "David's father. I had to come back to town for a couple of days, and I promised Dave I'd look you up. Now that I have — how about having dinner with me tonight and getting acquainted? I think we've both got things to talk about."

She did not not know what to say. She did not quite believe what was happening.

"I've already asked your grandmother. She thinks it would be very nice."

She looked at Gram. Gram nodded.

"I think it would be very nice too," he said. "How about it? Would you like to?"

There was something about him, in his smile, but most of all in the way he talked, that was just like David.

"Yes," she said.

Chapter 13

*I*T was called The Ancient Mariner, and it was like pictures she had seen of inns hundreds of years old.

The walls inside were of dark paneling; the ceiling was all rough-hewn beams. There were glowing candles on the tables and in ship's lamps around the walls. The whole room seemed alive in warmly flickering candlelight. Mr. Pinkham seemed to know everybody, and there was a lot of laughing and hand-shaking and being introduced to people whose names she promptly forgot.

After she had checked her coat, Mr. Pinkham said, "If you want to make up a little, the powder room is in there. I'll wait for you."

She was quite made up already and she didn't have to go to the room, but she went anyway because it seemed to be expected of her. She washed her hands, dried them and glanced in the mirror. It was a long time since she had consciously looked at herself; it was a little startling. The girl looking back at her had long, softly brushed fair hair; it seemed remarkably blonde in contrast with the simple, navy blue dress with its white collar and white sleeve trim. The girl was taller than she remembered her, very pale and solemn. She looked as though she had been ill; there were definite dark circles under her eyes. But in a strange sort of way she looked pretty too. She touched the dark circles with a curious fingertip, but there was nothing to be done about them.

She returned to the lobby. Mr. Pinkham took her hand and led her to the dining room. A man with a sheaf of menus in his hand said, "Any particular place, Don?"

"How about something by the big window?"

The man led them to a table, drew out a chair for her and slipped it under her when she sat down. Mr. Pinkham sat opposite her.

"Something to drink before you order?" the man asked.

Mr. Pinkham nodded. "Scotch here. Water." He glanced at Vanessa. "Would you like a little wine, Vanessa?"

"I don't know. Should I?"

"I think it would be nice. Make it port, Jim. A small one."

"Will do."

"Port's a nice wine," Mr. Pinkham explained. "Sweet. I think you'll like it, and it won't hurt you a bit."

She smiled nervously.

"Do you like fish?"

She nodded.

"Good. Because this is one of the few places away from the coast where you get really good fish. Just between you and me, I'd try the scrod — they ship it in fresh daily — or you might like the Fisherman's Platter. That's shrimp and sole and scallops. Either one, you can't miss."

He went on talking, as easily as though they had known each other for years and years. When the waitress came to take their order she smiled at Vanessa. "I didn't know you had a daughter, Don."

He shook his head. "No luck that way. This is Vanessa, she's an old friend of the family."

It was nice the way he had said it. His smile had been

109

nice too. In a funny, teasing kind of way, it had reminded her of David. When she ordered, she looked thoughtfully at the menu — even though she already knew what she was going to have — and tried to appear very calm and grown-up about it. "I'll have the scrod," she said. "And french fries."

"What would you like on the salad?"

That threw her. She looked at Mr. Pinkham.

"Have the house dressing," he said. "It's good."

"I'll have that," she agreed.

At the time it was happening, it was all so strange, so much like a dream that everything Mr. Pinkham talked about seemed to be passing through her. She knew that he was talking and that she was making proper responses, but that was really all. Only when it was over, and she was home and in bed, did she realize that everything had remained with her. Especially everything about David.

Most especially how Mr. Pinkham, with the table cleared except for their coffees, had looked down at the table and begun playing with a spoon, tracing aimless squiggles with it on the tablecloth.

"What it comes down to, Vanessa," he said, "is that I owe you a lot. A great deal more than I can ever repay. I mean about David." He sketched intently at the tablecloth. "He's a strange boy, you know. And this life he's been living with me, ramming around the country, it hasn't helped things much. He's a loner by nature, he's not one to make friends. And living the way we do, it's been a torn-up life for him. Maybe even if he wanted to make friends, he couldn't have. He was always being pulled away from places, schools. I think, in the past few years, he was slowly being pulled away from me. He went his way, I went mine. But his was a lonely way. And it got lonelier all the time. Maybe that's why the bird thing was so big with him. The birds never changed; wherever we moved there were birds to study. They were something he could give himself to. He was always better with birds and animals than people. Until he met you.

"I have the feeling, Vanessa, that you were maybe the first real friend he ever had. And he responded to it. I can't tell you — I can't possibly tell you what it did for him. And what it did was . . ."

He stopped for a few moments and said nothing. He just drew on the tablecloth. "Maybe the simplest way to say it is that he became a human being, not a mixed-up, defensive kid. He began to be the nice boy that had been locked up inside him for years, the boy I didn't know myself. Because of you, your friendship together."

He looked at her then, for the first time, and said very gravely. "What I really owe you, Vanessa — what I think I'm trying to say and not saying it too well — is that I owe you my son. You gave David back to me. How do I thank you for something like that? There's no way, none at all. Except to say thank you — so very much."

There was that.

And then there was the package Mr. Pinkham handed her when he took her up to the porch. "David wanted you to have this," he said. "I asked him to put a note in, although I'd be awfully surprised if he did. But if he didn't, it's not because he didn't care, or didn't want to. It's the reverse, if anything. You see, he's still a strange boy in many ways. And one of those ways is that he can't talk about — he simply can't talk about things that mean the most to him. I hope some day he changes, but right now that's the way he is. So please forgive him, and don't be too disappointed in case."

There was no note.

There were only the binoculars and the Peterson bird guide.

Which no longer mattered to her anymore.

She didn't know why she was doing it. She didn't even want to.

It was probably because it was just another Saturday with nothing to do and this would be something different, that was all. She slipped the binoculars around her neck, tucked the Peterson and a notebook in her jacket pocket and went down into The Bottoms. It was a mild afternoon, the sun was out full, and the woods were already greening. It was all outside her, though; it stopped at her skin. Inside her was the coldness that nothing, not even Mr. Pinkham's visit, had changed. She shivered in the coldness.

She did try to free herself from it, though. She looked at the trees and tried to feel the green haze of leaves about her, but they were merely trees and leaves. The field was merely weeds coming up. When she looked down into the pit from the dike, she saw the two lakes, the marshes, the cracked, shining plains of mud. She kept looking at them, trying to feel them, wanting to feel them, but feeling nothing. She closed her eyes and whispered inside herself, "Please let it come back, let it be the way it was." But when she opened them nothing had changed. What was there had nothing to say to her.

What was there once was gone.

She walked slowly around the top of the dike trying to find it. In the end, she knew that she shouldn't have come. And that she would never come again.

And then something — a faint sound she realized she had been hearing for some time — seemed to pierce her skin. It drove into her like a nail through ice.

A plaintive sound, sharp, thin, from somewhere along the shore of the large lake. She looked in the direction from which it had come. Saw nothing. But waited, listening.

It came again: *weet-weet*. Closer, but this time from a direction opposite from where it had been before. She turned toward it, her body suddenly no longer a wall between her and things, but a channel — a single, vibrating sense concentrated into listening. She was aware of the blue of the sky, the smell of wet spring earth, the sun-drenched wind burning into the frozen waste inside her. It was as though David had quietly remarked. "You have to allow for the wind flow around the dike, it confuses sounds." She waited, straining her ears. The sound came again. She raised the glasses and focused.

And there it was!

Almost invisible against the wet brown mud: a spotted sandpiper. Impossible to miss. She didn't need to look at the guidebook. And then — unbelievable! — only a little way beyond it another sandpiper, both moving slowly, bills dabbing into the mud, feeding. She lowered herself to the dike, careless of the mud, and watched them.

Something stirred in her. Began to function.

She glanced at her wrist watch. Two-thirty. She jotted the time in her notebook. The date. The weather, clear; temperature, mid-sixties; wind, southwest twelve to fifteen mph. Then the entry: two spotted sandpipers, north shore of large lake. She did these things automatically, as though she had never ceased doing them. Looking up from the notebook, she became aware of sound. Where she had heard nothing before, now from everywhere in The Bottoms was swelling an immense singing: shrills of redwings, piercings of song sparrows, yells of jays, rainsongs of robins, mewings of gulls sliding down the river. She began focusing on them, counting, recording, filling page after page in the notebook.

The afternoon slipped away.

It was nearing five o'clock when she picked her way down the bank of the dike and started back through The Bottoms.

She walked slowly, thinking.

There was a lot to do now. She had made a good start today, but it was only a start. She would come back again tomorrow and, after that, every weekend until school was out. And then every day through the summer, just like last year. Not because of David, although that was an important reason for doing it. But because she wanted to. This was her project now, and if it was going to have any value it would have to be done right.

Not that it hadn't been done right last summer. David had known what he was doing and he had been a wonderful teacher. But she had learned things too. And now that the project was hers, she saw that it could be done better. Because David, good as he was, had often been lazy and careless. He had never been very good at organizing himself or his time. So she would organize differently. She would divide The Bottoms into specific areas and keep separate notebooks on each. She would give much more attention to daily cycles and the behavior patterns of birds in each.

She would . . .

There was also something else she would have to do. There were the lost months of schoolwork to make up. They would have to be made up and there wasn't much time. But she could do it, perhaps, if she tried hard enough. And she would try. There was nothing preventing her now. The winter inside her was over at last and gone; she could still feel the afternoon sun deep in her skin. She wanted, for the first time in so long, to begin to try.

Gram was on the porch, her face filled with worry, when she dashed up the walk. "Vannie," she cried, "we've been so worried. Where have you been?"

Vanessa flung her arms around her and hugged her tightly.

"Home, Gram," she said. "Just home."

It seemed the most natural word in the world to say.

Epilogue

*T*HE driver opened the door of the bus and turned to the crowd pushing up the aisle. "Take your time, folks. Don't hurry. The ocean will still be there when you get out." He glanced at Vanessa, who was sitting directly behind him. "Wait till they're off. I'll get your bag down for you."

Vanessa nodded.

"Ever been to the Cape before?"

She shook her head.

"Well . . ."? He pointed outside; it was as though he were introducing her to what lay beyond. "This is Provincetown, P-Town we call it around here. The end of the line. Nothing beyond here but the old Atlantic."

She looked out of the window. There was nothing but buildings and shops, and people getting off the bus and people meeting them.

"Where you from?" he asked.

"Toledo," she managed to say.

"Never heard of it. Where's that?" She looked at him, startled; her eyes seemed larger than her face. Then she saw the glint in his eyes and knew he was teasing her. She forced a wan smile.

She was very frightened.

"Come all the way by bus?"

"I flew to Boston. Then I took the bus."

"I take it somebody's meeting you."

She swallowed. "Some friends."

He eased out from behind the wheel and stood up. "Go ahead. I'll bring your bag."

She got off the bus. A moment later the driver set her bag beside her. "Good luck, kid," he said, and pushed through the crowd.

She waited, looking around, slowly beginning to panic.

All at once a pair of hands on her shoulders turned her around and she looked up into an immense grin.

"Vanessa!"

The panic was suddenly gone. "Mr. Pinkham."

"I see you got the tickets all right."

She nodded dumbly.

"There's a big lummox around here somewhere dying to see you." He glanced around. "Hey, Dave!" He pointed. "There he is. I'll take your bag, Vanessa. Dave can bring you to the car."

And suddenly there he was!

Tanned, as always. A shy, awkward smile on his face. In fact, if it hadn't been for the smile she might not have recognized him at once. He was taller than she remembered — he seemed to have shot up two or three inches — and he was wearing a black blazer and gray trousers. She had never seen him dressed up before. He looked at her.

"Vannie," he said.

"Hello, David."

She did not know what to do. He did not seem to know what to do either. He thrust out his hand and she took it. It was very cold. They kept holding hands, neither wanting to be the first to let go.

117

Suddenly he said, "Oh, the hell with it," and the next moment his arms were around her in a huge bear hug. "Vannie, you bum, you."

She laughed delightedly.

"Listen," he said, letting her go and taking her arm. "How are things at the pit? Have you been keeping up the records? Did the sandpipers come back?"

"The spotteds did."

"They'd have come anyway. But the others, the dunlins, the leasts? On time? How do things look compared with last year? How about the herons and egrets? Listen, we're going to have fun. We've got gulls here you've never seen before. As soon as we get to Wellfleet — that's just down the road — we'll go out to the beach and . . ."

But she wasn't listening or caring anything at all about what he was saying.

She was just happy, trudging along with him arm in arm to the waiting car.

7033